MY AWESOME PLACE

THE AUTOBIOGRAPHY of CHERYL B

TOPSIDE
SIGNATURE
NEW YORK

Topside Signature
228 Park Avenue South, #14261, New York, NY 10003
www.topsidesignature.com

Burke, Cheryl, 1972-2011

My awesome place: the autobiography of Cheryl B / Burke, Cheryl.

ISBN 978-0-9832422-4-6 (hardcover)
ISBN 978-0-9832422-5-3 (paperback)
ISBN 978-0-9832422-6-0 (ebook)
LCCN 2012951032

10 9 8 7 6 5 4 3 2 1

First Edition
Cover and interior design by Julie Blair

This book is dedicated to the
City of New York, for helping
so many people find their
awesome place.

MY AWESOME PLACE

THE AUTOBIOGRAPHY of CHERYL B

Acknowledgements

That this book was completed is a testament to the generous contributions of the members Cheryl Burke's writers group, Anne Elliott, Virginia Vitzthum, Maria Luisa Tucker, as well the editorial guidance of Sarah Schulman and Kathleen Warnock. Additionally, support from Kelli Dunham, Stephanie Schroeder and Nicole Fox was invaluable during the publication process.

Ultimately, there are hundreds of names who should be credited here, people who supported and encouraged Cheryl's work during the nearly 20 years she was writing and performing in New York City and around the world. *My Awesome Place* is truly the result of a massive community effort to honor her work in a meaningful and lasting way.

MY AWESOME PLACE
THE AUTOBIOGRAPHY of CHERYL B

Foreword

CHERYL BURKE DIED OF MEDICAL MALPRACTICE IN JUNE 2011 AT the age of 38. A standard course of chemo for Hodgkin's Lymphoma resulted in profound damage to her lungs, and after months of suffering and hospitalizations, her life ended at Beth Israel Hospital in New York City, in the presence of her loving partner Kelli Dunham.

Cheryl was a very beloved member of the writing, performance and queer communities in New York and internationally, and a personal friend. When she died she left a working draft of this manuscript. Members of her writing group lovingly combed their notes and emails to reconstruct as much of the book as they could, and made it possible for us to have this precious treasure of her life finally sit on our shelves.

When I was editing their notes, Kelli sent me this very emblematic sample from Cheryl's blog:

I was at a VERY fancy literary party in a high-class loft in Manhattan. I was there early and I stood in the kitchen talking to a fellow writer, I'll call him "Dude."

Dude's friend walked into the apartment wearing a flannel shirt and a wool cap. Dude called out to his friend, "What are you wearing? You look like a low life."

The friend took off his hat and said, "what?"

"I said you look like a low life," Dude said, "like a longshoreman or something."

Now, Dude had no idea my father was a longshoreman, so I didn't take this as an insult. Indeed the friend definitely did look like a smaller, gay version of my dad in his work clothes. Dude had probably never known blue-collar people and probably didn't think any of their progeny would be at this type of event. It probably did not occur to him that describing a longshoreman, as a "low life" may have been offensive to his present company. I didn't know what to say, so I turned my attention to a bowl of hummus. I didn't even blog about it at the time, thinking perhaps I was making too much of the situation. But looking back at it now, this experience exemplifies the two worlds I've been teetering between since I left my parents' house to go to college all those years ago; my uneducated working class family and the more intellectual and in some cases, overeducated and overly entitled circles I now run with. And the fact that I've pretty much always felt like an outsider to both."

Although she felt alienated, Cheryl spoke to a lot of people's experiences of not fitting in, passing for middle-class, writing into elite systems from the outside. And she showed enormous empathy personally by encouraging younger and emerging writers, recognizing older ones and treating everyone with respect regardless of their social position. As a curator she facilitated a wide range of writers from different levels, experiences and aesthetics and treated them with kindness and inclusion. The dramatic story recounted in *My Awesome Place* combined with the ever insightful, open-hearted, deadpan world view, brings the readers close to the true Cheryl, loved and valued by her friends. Her aesthetic lived in that juxtaposition of humor and honesty, which is what helped her live, love and write until her final days.

SARAH SCHULMAN

1

Winter Wonderland

THE DECEMBER AIR IS COLD, THE SKY A MIDNIGHT BLUE. I'm standing in the archway of my parents' split-level ranch home poking my fingers through the holes in the screen door and watching as the darkened exterior of each neighbor's house lights up with holiday cheer.

A shrub in front of the house next door morphs into a snowman complete with a crooked, demonic grin. Santa's sled becomes eerily illuminated on a rooftop a few houses down. Across the street, three skeletal wise men lurch forward like zombies. The whole scene is really intense and I'm not sure how much of that has to do with the tiny joint I just devoured in my bedroom, carefully blowing the smoke out my window or how much is simply the utter absurdity of the Christmas season. The outside of our house is not decorated in its usual fashion—lots of lights and gigantic candy canes—out of respect for my grandmother who died in November. But my mother's heavily armored Christmas tree still stands by the corner window in the living room. For years now, I have refused to help decorate or even acknowledge the tree, out of my distaste for all things traditional and excessive.

In my pocket is a tiny blue tab of acid waiting to invade my bloodstream. I tenderly rub it back and forth between my thumb and forefinger as if it were a fine jewel ready to be presented to my beloved.

But I am an obese sixteen-year-old suburban girl with no hope of romance—two hundred and thirty pounds of pure anti-sex. Then there are my parents, who don't want me to go to college and my loathsome guidance counselor who suggested I should look into a career as a toll taker on the New Jersey Turnpike.

"It would be a good job for someone like you," Ms. O'Hare said when I presented her with a list of colleges to which I wanted to apply. "Face it, you're not really college material."

I wonder what she meant by "someone like me". Did she mean a fat chick? The daughter of a longshoreman? Then again, what did I know about college anyway? No one in my family had ever gone. Perhaps Ms. O'Hare, as much as I hated her, was right. And her comments the other day were a none-too-subtle way of telling me the truth; that "someone like me" was a total loser.

I hastily swallow the acid and run to the bathroom, turn on the tap, cup my hands below the running water and drink. I lean toward the mirror and study my forehead. I've often been told that I have perfect skin, which I would eagerly trade with any of the acne-riddled girls I know for their thin, shapely bodies.

I move farther away and regard my entire reflection. "This is the face of someone who is too poor, stupid and fat to go to college." I begin to feel claustrophobic thinking about the toll booth, the polyester uniform stretched tight across my stomach.

When I break out in a cold sweat, I know the acid is beginning its fantastic journey. The clock in the hallway tells me it is 7:30 before it melts and disappears into a tiny hole in the wall.

Jean was supposed to pick me up at 7. I was supposed to climb into the passenger side of her old, dirty-white Toyota Corolla and we were supposed to drive to the parking lot of the Sheraton hotel in front of my development where we would take the acid.

We would then drive to Mark and Sarah's house. Mark and Sarah live in Sarah's mom's basement. They are older, 19, and the fact that they are married makes them seem so mature. Sarah's mom would descend upon us at 2 a.m. holding a tray of freshly baked cookies, and I would think she was the coolest mom ever. Sarah however, would be embarrassed by her mother's hipness, her stories about Woodstock, her complete and total approval of our drug use.

I make my way out to the living room and flop onto my favorite velveteen chair, rub the material back and forth, leaving a trail of fingers on the surface. It feels soft going one way and rough the other. I rub harder, "soft, rough, soft, rough, soft, rough..." I am saying this out loud now, working it into a chant. Coco, the dog comes and sits by my chair. So I transfer my rubbing to him saying, "brown doggie, brown doggie." He loves it, rolls over on his back. I keep rubbing his belly, "oh, you're a fluffy dog, a fluffy dog."

And before I know it, a shadowy figure is approaching us. It's the mothership and she lands before me. Coco gets up and slinks away. So much for a best friend.

"Are you drunk?" My mother asks, tapping her foot on the carpet. "Have you been drinking beer?"

I just look at her.

"I can't believe it, you're drunk."

I get up and turn toward the window, and that's when I notice it: the tree, dripping in lights, satin-covered Styrofoam balls, glass icicles, crocheted snowmen, the entire casts of *Snow White* and *Lady and the Tramp* dangling off of 8 feet of fake fir. It glistens with decadence, and a tiny motor in the base slowly rotates the tree as the lights flash on and off, while an internal tape player spews forth "White Christmas." Atop the entire mess sits a blond, blue-eyed porcelain angel dressed in a baptismal gown.

I move closer to the tree, so close, it becomes a blur of lights and colors moving slowly before me like a kaleidoscope.

My mother stands behind, in awe, "I can't believe you're looking at the tree." She calls out to my father: "She's looking at the tree."

My father shouts back, half-asleep, from his recliner in the basement, "What do you want? I'm busy."

"She's looking at the tree! Come quick," my mother says.

I am not just looking at the tree, I am communing with it. I am studying its elements, its nuances.

The fathership lands. He is also standing behind me next to my mother. It's rare that they stand together in any manner.

"Is she drunk?" my father asks, irritated.

"Oh, I'm so excited. She likes the tree! I'm going to get the camera!" My mother has forgotten about my being "drunk" but my father turns me around.

"Have you been drinking my Budweiser?" He asks.

He looks directly into my eyes. My pupils must be the size of quarters by now, but he says nothing, doesn't even seem to notice. My parents are not schooled in the ways of narcotics. As he studies me, he moves closer, trying to catch a whiff of my breath.

The last time we stood this close, a few weeks before, he slapped my face after I tried to slit my wrists. I went into the bathroom, took out some razors and start cutting myself. My brother saw me go in there and somehow knew what I was doing.

He yelled out, "Cheryl's trying to commit suicide in the bathroom!"

My father knocked the door off its hinges in one try. This is not the first time he's knocked a door down. He is good at this. He chased me from the bathroom back to my room, grabbed me by the back of my neck and put my head through the wall. By the time he threw me on my bed and hurled a glass-encased picture of mauve flowers (my mother had decided to decorate my room in mauve) across the room we were both covered in my blood. I reached over and picked up a piece of broken glass, threatening to further cut my arms with it. My father was enraged. He slapped me so hard I heard something crack when my head turned.

My mother came in, told my father I'd had enough. Then she told me to wash the blood off my hands. She said I'll be okay. She was too embarrassed to take me to the hospital. I looked at the hole in the paneling on the wall and realize it is right next to the spot my father had put my head through four years earlier. My parents had paneled over the wall, which was thin and flimsy, and I could see the original entry point and for some reason that made me crack up.

In the now, tripping, I look hard at my father, it seems as if his eyes have combined into one large eye in the middle of his brow. I want tell him *no, I didn't drink your goddamn beer* but I just can't find the words so instead I shake my head.

"Good, that stuff's expensive," my father says then turns and walks away.

My mother returns with the camera.

"Wait, don't go! She's looking at the tree, we have to get a picture."

I still don't turn around, but my mother starts snapping anyway.

My father's name is Bob, short for Robert. When his friends call the house they ask for "Snapper." That was his nickname from the old neighborhood. Apparently all the men from the old neighborhood in Staten Island had nicknames.

When I answer the phone and it's for him, I call out, "Snapper, you got a phone call." And he would always say to my mother, "Don't let her call me that." He hardly ever addresses me directly. He's really awkward like that. My mother calls him Snapper as well. The moniker became a mystery for me to solve.

As a teenager, I was determined to find out what the nickname meant. My mother wouldn't tell me, and my father and I didn't talk much. I looked through his drawers and found a broken statue of St. Anthony, an old flask, a pocketknife, pictures of his parents and a small box of bullets—he didn't own a gun. I thought perhaps the name had to do with fishing. My father loved fishing, kept a garage full of fishing accoutrements, maybe he caught a lot of snapper. He did win trophies for catching the largest striped bass on the East Coast. But deep down, I knew it probably had nothing to do with fish and was perhaps something less savory.

I'd heard in bits and pieces over the years that the crew from the old neighborhood were bad boys: there was some small time thievery, aimless hanging on street corners, disrespect of women. I don't know which of these my father may have been guilty of, my mother won't tell me. But as a group I guess they had a reputation.

Sometimes I picture my father as a youth: looking like an Irish John Travolta from the movie "Grease," hanging with his posse, wearing a leather jacket, stealing hubcaps, and using a lot of toothpicks.

He had an eighth-grade education and a short temper. He smoked two packs of Marlboros a day (since he was twelve), and styled his thick, black hair with generous amounts of pomade.

I remember being five years old and sitting on my father's lap. I rubbed my hand across his cheek and repeated a line I must have heard on a TV commercial: "I love a man with a clean, close shave."

My father, who had barely any facial hair to begin with, laughed so hard I almost fell off his lap. He called my mother over, "Hey Phyllis, check this out!"

He had me do it again. She also burst out laughing.

This became my trick. When company came, my father would say, "Cher, do that thing with my face." I would climb into his lap and repeat the trick. The audience always thought it was the funniest thing. And I was young enough to want to please the adults by whatever means necessary, devoid of pride, embarrassment or cynicism.

"You better put her in a convent!" they would joke. "She's already crazy for the men."

I remember being embarrassed, pretty sure this comment had something to do with S-E-X. S-E-X was the reason why my father didn't want me watching The Dallas Cowboys Cheerleaders. "I don't want her to get any ideas," I heard him say.

I had to go stand in the kitchen as my mother, father and little brother Greg watched them on the TV in the living room. I could come back in when the cheerleaders were done.

There was a lot of talk about putting girls into convents although I don't remember anyone actually being sent to one. It was more of a thin, absurd threat that hung in the air between precocious daughters and their wary parents.

When my family moved to New Jersey, we moved to a town called Holmdel, one of the richest in the Garden State. Before we even set up house, we realized we didn't belong. We moved because my father's childhood friend, who managed to become a millionaire selling computers even though he knew nothing about computers, was planning on moving here. My father idolized his friend and always compared our family to his. We were never good enough.

As we unpacked our belongings, we christened ourselves "The Holmdel Hillbillies," because of our ramshackle cars. One was a green Duster my father had since before I was born; another was a no-name Sixties-style sedan in a dead beige given to us by my father's aunts. Aunt Ann and Julia also lent my parents the money for the house.

We moved to what was considered the "poor" section of Holmdel, which means it was perfectly middle class, with three-bedroom, one-and-a-half bath split-level houses on half-acre plots of land. Our immediate neighbors seemed to have newer, nicer cars and other parts of town serve as virtual luxury car showcases.

As we are a family that thrives on self-deprecation, we are happy with our identity as hillbillies.

Our development is behind the Sheraton Hotel, off of Highway 35, exit 117 on the Garden State Parkway. After we move in, for the first time in my life, I ride a yellow bus to school. On Staten Island I walked the few blocks to school every day. In New Jersey, I attend public school, whereas before I went to Catholic school. The change makes me very happy, but poses another problem: I have nothing to wear and I'm fat. I beg my parents for designer jeans. I don't own any other jeans, just two pairs of tent-like corduroys, but all the girls have designer jeans: Jordache, Sergio Valente, Gloria Vanderbilt. I wanted the Sergios, dark blue with turquoise piping. I discovered there was a designer jeans store across the street from my house. I spent many afternoons trying to squeeze into a pair. It never worked: my stomach was just too big, even the largest men's sizes wouldn't do the trick. As much as I hated wearing the plaid Catholic school uniform with saddle shoes, at least I didn't really have to think about it.

One day my father called me down to the family room. He was in his recliner with the TV on. He pointed at the screen where a condom commercial was playing.

"Ya see that?" He asked.

"Yes, I see it," I answered, a bit embarrassed.

"Ya see that?" he repeated.

The people in the commercial were riding horses through a field one second, cuddling on a couch the next.

"Yes, sure do," I said.

"You know what that is?" He looked at me with a combination of curiosity and accusation.

"Yes, I do know."

"You understand what I'm talking about?" He continued to interrogate me.

I was 17 by then and well-accustomed to the Dad shorthand. I understood this was his attempt at teaching me the birds and the bees.

"Yes, I believe so," I said.

"You got it?" he persisted, the commercial was over, but he still pointed at the TV screen.

"Yes, got it. Thanks."

"Good," he said, then changed the channel and silently dismissed me.

This was a typical conversation between us: nothing is said and everything is inferred. I didn't tell him that I had already purchased my own not-yet-used condoms.

I didn't remind him that I've known about condoms

since I was a little girl when I found a box of them in the glove compartment of his car.

My mother and I were in his car, a small, red thing, rusted with age. I was about nine and on my way to dance class. My mother navigated the narrow, winding streets of Staten Island to Mrs. Rosemary's Dance Academy and I played with the latch on the bright pink bag that held my dance shoes, moving the small piece of metal in and out until my mother yelled, "For Chrissakes, can you please stop that!"

I stopped and began to look through my father's glove compartment for gum. I poked through a mess of papers and emergency flares—my father kept an inordinate number of emergency flares in his glove compartment—until I came across a small box, about the same size as a package of Pop Rocks. It had already been opened and the flap was tucked back in. A romantic scene was shown on the front of the package: two silhouettes burned a crimson-tinged yellow in the sunset. The woman had straight, long, dirty-blond hair, blown slightly in the breeze, the trace of a smile on her face. The man was solid, with a firm jaw. He had his arms wrapped around the woman. I poked my finger into the package and out popped two connected squares of plastic. On the clear side there were two protruding rings in a clear liquid. The other side was an orangey hue with the words "ribbed for her pleasure" emblazoned over and over in perfectly straight lines as if, for punishment, someone's teacher had made them stay after school to complete this task. I squished the liquid around in the package, making the ring move back and forth. As my mother made a sharp right turn onto a busy two-way street, a car pulled out in front of us and she swerved. My mother cursed and instinctually threw her arm out in front of me, shielding me from any impact.

"I hate this traffic," she added. The adults in my life were always complaining; complaining about the weather, the traffic, the heating bills, their spouses and kids. Life seemed like one long string of misery and discontent.

"What are these, Mommy?" I asked, holding up the condoms.

My mother looked over at what I was holding, her eyes widened and her brow furrowed. "Where did you find those?"

"In the glove compartment."

"Put them down!"

"What are they?"

"They're very dirty things."

They looked pretty clean to me, but I dropped them on the floor anyway. Suddenly, my mother slammed on the brakes, made a U-turn and gunned it back to our house.

"What are you doing? I have to go to dancing school."

She didn't answer. She didn't say anything until we pulled up in front of our house, then grabbed the small box, yanked me out of the car and pulled me up our walkway. We burst into the house to find my father and my little brother Greg sprawled on the floor, watching TV. My mother threw the box at my father, hitting him on the forehead.

"Your daughter wants to know what these are!"

"Where'd you get these?" My father demanded. He looked at me as if it were my fault.

"They were in your car, you son of a bitch." My mother answered.

"What were you doing in my glove compartment?" he screamed at my mother.

"Your daughter was in there. Not me."

"I was looking for gum." I offered.

"Well, don't go in there anymore," he told me.

"Come on Bob, aren't you going to tell her what they are? Huh? Huh?" my mother egged him.

They continued to fight for the rest of the afternoon resorting to a series of accusations that Greg and I could not understand. They never answered my question. And it would be years until I figured out why my mother was so mad that he kept condoms in his car.

The people from the condom box became active players in my dreams. The man would approach the woman holding a fluorescent emergency flare: "Here, this is for your pleasure." The woman would blush, flick her hair and take the offering in her hand. "Thanks!" They would kiss and walk off into the sunset. I couldn't understand what kind of pleasure those little plastic squares could possibly give anyone.

I also had dreams in which I ate them and they tasted like sour rubber.

When I started having sex in my seventeenth year, I purchased the same brand of condoms and eventually grew cavalier enough to keep them in my glove compartment, as if I were carrying on some demented, unspoken family tradition.

My father had a "workshop" in our garage that he lorded over with an almost comic passion, since he seemed unable to fix anything. When we moved to New Jersey, the workshop consisted of old kitchen cabinets and a long counter, moved from our former residence on Staten Island. The cabinets were drilled together in the back to form a straight row along one wall. The counter was adorned with a scary-looking anvil that had snapped up my brother's or my fingers on more than one occasion. Like most of his tools, I don't think he ever used the anvil. He forbid us to be in or around his workshop much less for fear of us getting hurt, I think, than that he thought of it as his private place.

My father's decade-long quest to fix the roof only resulted in him mooning the entire neighborhood the first day of every Spring. My brother and I called this annual phenomenon "Full Moon Over Miller Avenue." He was a big guy; 6'4" and close to 300 pounds. He ordered his clothes from a Big & Tall catalog. Most of his weight was in his stomach, which spilled out from the front of his jeans. His pants were always too big in the back and despite the belt he used to keep them up, they always slid down.

There was a patch of roof on the upper right hand corner of our split-level ranch that was in constant need of repair. Each year, my father would set out when the weather was agreeable, place the ladder on the side of the house and climb up to the roof with a box of tools and a bucket of white, wet, stuff. As soon as he bent over to start work, his jeans would slip, a little at first then slowly they would inch down until after about twenty minutes they reached what we called the "half-crack" line. Then we'd get a call from Teresa, our 60-year old neighbor across the street, who could often be found sitting on her front lawn in a bikini.

"Phyllis," Teresa hissed into the phone, exhaling a long line of cigarette smoke. "I can see your husband's ass."

Teresa's pool, which was hidden behind a tall wooden fence, had mythical qualities for me. I'd heard it was a beautiful oasis surrounded by trees and alabaster statues. I never saw the pool, as it was her habit to invite only men into her chlorine-infused lair. On one memorable occasion, Teresa tried to entice several of the boys who were arriving for my brother's 14th birthday party, but no one's curiosities were piqued enough to discover what lay on the other side of Teresa's wood-clad fortress.

After Teresa's call, we would go outside and my mother would shout up at my father "for Chrissakes Bob. Get down. Everyone can see your ass."

My father would answer, brandishing his hammer, "Who's gonna fix this roof? Huh? Are you going to fix it? Are the kids going to fix it?"

"We have to hire someone," my mother would shout at him.

"Who's going to pay for that? Huh? You? The kids?"

He would begin his descent from the roof, cursing and stomping his way back to the house. "Is there anything to eat? Come on, I've been working all day. I'm hungry," he would say, dropping his tools on the counter in the workshop, pulling up his pants and slamming the screen door behind him.

When I was fifteen, my family went on a Disney cruise. This vacation brought together two of my least favorite things: the saccharine world of The Magic Kingdom and seasickness. As a cynical, morose, horny, depressed, petulant and obese teenager, this was the worst thing that could happen to me.

The excursion was made worse by the fact that my after school job had helped. How did I know when I signed on to work at Roy Rogers for $4 an hour that they were owned by the Marriott Corporation? And how did I know that in the employee handbook, which I never read, it said that all employees of the Marriott Corporation receive a discount on Marriott hotels and package deals including those in The Magic Kingdom? And how did I know that if I left said employee handbook on the dining room table that my mother would actually read it then jump up and down in elation screaming, "we can finally afford to go on that Disney cruise!" But that's exactly what happened in the summer between my sophomore and junior year of high school. I had no choice in the matter, I was going to be cruising with Mickey and Minnie. And I thought I was working to save money to get away from my parents.

The first struggle involved baggage and not the metaphysical kind, My mother wanted to pack a "family suitcase" but I couldn't stand the thought of everyone else's clothes rubbing up against mine. I pulled together socks, t-shirts, my one pair of plus-size jeans that fit properly, my two tent-like denim skirts and my Lane Bryant bikini underwear. Then there was the matter of my hair and makeup needs, which for a Jersey girl in the late 1980's was of no small import. There was a 16-inch can of Aqua Net, three different brushes, assorted scrunchies, bobby pins and barrettes. There were six different shades of Wet & Wild eye shadow; three different colors of mascara; charcoal, black and midnight blue eyeliners and a lighter with which to warm the eyeliner—it went on thicker and easier that way. There was the costume jewelry; the giant earrings, the garish, beaded necklaces, the sparkly rhinestone rings, multiple rubber and silver bracelets and the ankle charm bracelet. There was the purse with the flowers, the black leather bag with the snakeskin inlets, the metallic gold satchel.

There was my Walkman and an old ballet shoe box full of cassette tapes; there was the classic rock and the alternative rock, there was the heavy metal and the 70's disco. There was my only pair of stiletto heels, the wrestling shoes, the Converse All Stars. There was my teddy bear and a small, furry pillow to which I'd grown accustomed.

All except for the makeup, which I carried in a separate plastic box, fit into the large purple duffel bag I won at a fair in the fifth grade. The bag was decorated with unicorns on one side, and multiple Pegasuses on the other. It was all I had to keep my family's cooties off of my stuff.

When I descended the stairs carrying the bag and plastic box, my mother was quick to comment. "Well, if it isn't Madame Fifi with her own bag! Will Madame Fifi be dining with the family today or should I serve you your dinner in fucking bed?"

We were a cursing household, something that others often found alarming, and one of the things that often made our relatives refer to us as the Bundys (the fictional TV family on *Married with Children.*) Although we were really nothing like the Bundys, our dysfunction could be felt a mile away. When I imagined my parent's perfect teenage daughter, I picture Kelly Bundy in a convent.

Yes, I've been tripping. Still tripping. On the Christmas tree. Now I hear a car horn honking. It must be Jean.

I realize there is a bat flying overhead. I'm sure of it. I can hear its wings flapping. I look up and instead of a bat, it's the angel getting ready to take flight from atop the tree. (Later on, I realize this is another feature of the tree, the angel flaps its wings on each rotation.) But at that moment, the angel has become a white bat, looking right at me, about to dive into my hair. I grab one of the glass icicles for protection and hold it firmly.

My mother is still snapping pictures as I walk out the door. I look back at her. She is wearing a sweatshirt with a satin appliqué of a reindeer. The reindeer has an actual bell around its neck. These sweatshirts seem to be popular with all the mothers.

I head to the curb expecting to see Jean's white Corolla. Instead there is a monster truck blocking my parents' driveway. I can see Jean's teased blonde hair sitting tall on the driver's side. I climb the small stepladder attached to the side of the truck and make my way into the passenger seat. Jean is wearing micro, tight turquoise shorts and matching stiletto heels underneath a big white coat, the coat is open and flowing around her, exposing her perennially tanned legs. She looks annoyed as the monster truck screeches away from my house. I look back and silently say goodbye to my parents: one-eyed dad and reindeer mom.

Jean begins talking immediately: "This guy on the street just yelled at me, 'hey what's up with your boyfriend's truck' and I was like it's not my boyfriend's truck, and he's like 'okay, then your brother's truck,' I was like it's not my brother's truck asshole and then he's like 'tell your father he has a hot truck and a whore for a daughter.'"

"You should have run him over," I offer.

"I mean just because I'm a girl doesn't mean I can't have a truck."

"Totally," I say.

"I mean I'm liberated. Why can't I have my own truck?"

"Where did you get the truck?" I ask.

"That guy at the garage. The guy I'm seeing. He's fixing my car so he let me have the truck." She turns to face me and I can see the left side of her hair is kind of flat, her lipstick is a mess and she has a huge hickey on her neck.

"You should fix your lipstick," I say.

Jean looks in the rearview mirror as she makes a sharp turn. She is holding a cigarette in her right hand while she pops a tape into the player. Her left hand is on the steering wheel. Jean is not a good friend. I really don't have any good friends, just some friendly acquaintances. We both work at the hardware store and we both like classic rock and that's about all we have in common.

"Shit, it's totally fucked up, get out my makeup bag, it's in my purse on the floor by your feet."

I locate the makeup bag and hand it to her. I realize I've forgotten my purse, and with it all my makeup and my hairspray. I probably look like shit. I try to check myself out in the side mirror, then catch a glimpse of my stomach, bulging under the giant INXS concert t-shirt I'm wearing over spandex leggings and Converse hightops. I decide it doesn't matter what my face looks like; no amount of makeup can hide my biggest flaws.

Jen is staring at me, studying me. I wish she would keep her eyes on the road.

"Are you high?" she asks.

"Yes, sorry. I couldn't wait."

"We were supposed to do it together."

"I know. I'm sorry. It was really stupid. I had to sit there with my parents tripping my face off."

She pulls into an empty section of the parking lot in front of my development and parks across four spaces. First she applies pink lipstick, then fixes her hair. She takes out her tiny tab and swallows. She drinks from a bottle of Mountain Dew, leaving a fresh, pink ring on the opening, then offers me some. I'm not sure I can swallow so I shake my head.

Jean turns the truck around and pulls out onto the highway. She taps her fingers in time with the music and sings along. I can't seem to keep up. I watched Jean put the tape in so I know it's *Led Zeppelin 4*, but it sounds like one long gash of noise and not at all like the greatest album ever. Obviously, I am beyond the fun-loving portion of my trip and am entering the "will I ever be normal again?" leg. I hold onto my seat belt for dear life and methodically rub the material up and down.

I'm afraid of heights and being up in the monster truck is making me queasy. Any feeling of superiority I am supposed to get by being up so high and in an vehicle so large is negated by the unending vertigo I get from looking out the window onto the smaller, normal-sized cars. And of course I can't stop doing this. I keep glancing out the window as if on a dare.

And each time I think: *Will this be the one where the door swings open and I'll fall to my death from 10 feet at 70 miles an hour?*

Then I wish I was in one of the smaller cars or was one of the smaller cars. Then I realize this is just an allegory for my life; I am the oversized monster truck who just wants to be a normal mid-sized sedan.

I must look pretty intense, because Jean slaps me in the arm.

I quickly swing my head around, afraid I'd voiced some of my thoughts out loud.

Jean hasn't noticed my inner anguish and I don't realize she has stopped the truck in the middle of an unfamiliar street, also brightly lit up in the holiday spirit. She points to an animal sitting on someone's lawn, amongst a life-sized Nativity scene.

"A bunny?" I ask based on the white fur.

"No, it's a cat. It has two heads."

"You're fucking with me."

"No, really, look closer."

I zero in on the animal, get it into deep focus. There are definitely two heads, one atop the other, each making faces of excruciating pain. Years later, while watching a nature program that featured two lions mating, the male practically sitting on the female, their heads one atop the other, I had a flashback to the night in the monster truck and suddenly it all made sense. But in the moment, Jean and I are sure we have stumbled upon one of Satan's minions.

"Do you think it's a sign?" she asks, "Like of the end of the world?" The first side of the tape finishes and Jean mechanically takes it out, flips it over and pushes it back in.

"Do we just leave it there?" she asks.

"Yes, we leave it there. It might have rabies."

"Are you sure?"

"Yes. Let's go to Mark and Sarah's."

"We can't. Mark came onto me the last time we were there."

"Really?" I don't remember anything like that happening. Why doesn't anybody come on to me?

"And Sarah's really jealous." Jeanette says and successfully attempts a K-turn in the middle of the narrow street.

I look down at my fat body, my tattered olive-green tent coat purchased off the sale rack at the Limited 2 years ago. My chipped nail polish and chapped hands. I would never make another girl jealous.

We drive by the two-headed cat three more times just to make sure we really saw what we saw. The first time the two heads are still there. The second time only one head remains.

"What do you think happened to the other head?" Jean asks. It is obvious she has entered the "is this ever going to end?" segment of her trip.

"Maybe the remaining head ate it."

The third time we drive by there is no cat at all, no sign that a cat with any number of heads had ever been there.

We spend most of the night driving from one nearby town to the next in search of more mutant animals. We don't find any so we stop by the monster truck guy's house where he and Jeanette disappear into the bedroom and I am deposited in front of the TV like a child begrudgingly baby-sat, with a forty of Budweiser and an endless supply of *Magnum P.I.* re-runs on video. Monster truck guy even apologizes to me for not having any snacks. I am still wearing my coat and I reach into the pocket to find the glass icicle. I squeeze it hard in my hand, trying to make it shatter, but it won't budge. I put the icicle on the table and try to smash it with the beer bottle, still nothing. I step on it, throw it against the wall, sit on it. It just won't die. I open the front door and throw it out into the night. That's when it begins to snow.

2

Jersey Shore

MY BEDROOM DOOR HADN'T CLOSED IN YEARS, EVER SINCE MY father busted it down during an argument in the seventh grade. Six years later, the summer after my freshman year of college, it remained broken.

My mother pushed her way into the room, a cigarette dangling from her lips. "You're coming with me!" she grabbed my arm. "I'm not doing this alone!"

"What the fuck?" I shook her off. I'd been sitting atop my bed, waiting until it was time to leave for my shift at Rickels Home Center, where I'd worked during high school. I was re-reading *The Catcher in the Rye* and wondering if I'd be getting enough financial aid to return to NYU in the fall.

"He wants to fuck some whore," she exhaled some smoke. "I want his daughter to see him, that son of a bitch. Come on, get in the goddamn car!"

"I have to go to work in a few hours," I protested. I wanted nothing to do with my parent's marital problems—this was one of the reasons I left to begin with. I was determined to separate myself from them and surround myself with intellectuals. That's why I went to college, in New York City.

I learned early that separation was not so easy. My mother called me three to four times a day at least, leaving a series of messages all starting with the phrase, "Cheryl, it's yuh mutha." (She continued this phone habit throughout my college years and my early twenties. These four words became a saying and for years to come, friends would begin their conversations with this same line.) She pulled me out of bed, led me by the back of my neck down the stairs, and out the door.

"Get in the car!" she demanded.

I looked at my captor, who still held me the way a mother cat holds a kitten. "It's okay," I said, "I'm here. I'm not going to escape. You can let go of me."

I had come home for the summer at her insistence. "You're getting too independent," my phone stalker had told me toward the end of my second semester. I could hear her exhaling a line of smoke on the other end.

I climbed into the passenger seat. My mother dropped a bag in the back. I turned around and noticed it was open, spilling forth a pile of my father's clothes on top of which was his prized possession: his Members Only jacket.

"This is a designer jacket," my father would say to me, fondling his gold crucifix, and smelling like Old Spice. "You can dress it up or dress it down." It was 1991 and my father had worn this jacket since the early '80s.

My mutha filled me in with the rest of the details: My father hadn't been home for about a day and half. This happened often. It was what he had always referred to as "doing my thing." He'd been doing his thing for years, but my mother had just received word that my father and his friend were holed up in a condo down the shore with two women and that day she decided to stop having it.

I wanted to say something to make it better for her, but I didn't know what. My parents never got along. My mother lived with her strict Italian-American parents until she was 28 and got married. She had a sheltered life, then gave up a career on Wall Street, where she'd worked her way up from secretary to broker (with no college degree), when she married my father and later became pregnant with me. Both her parents and my father had pressured her to quit the job. "What kind of mother goes to work every day?" they said to her, "what kind of mother leaves her baby?"

When we got to the shore town, home to the purported adulterous hangout, we drove through row upon row of pastel-colored condos until we found their cars. My mother pulled up alongside my father's red Honda Civic and grabbed the garbage bag out of the backseat. She began dumping his clothes all over the Civic and screamed in the direction of the house, "you son of a bitch!"

My father emerged from behind a mint green door, followed by his friend.

"What's your problem? Huh?" My father asked. I probably should have gotten out of the car and kept my parents separated, but I was immobile.

"You think this is nice? Is this the way you want your daughter to see you?" she pointed at me. I shrank down in the seat. I hadn't been to the Jersey shore in over a year. As a fat teenager, I had found it to be an incredibly oppressive place. Even though I had lost a lot of weight since high school, I still felt constricted by ocean air. The condo neighborhood was eerily quiet, so my parents' voices carried high above the calls of the seagulls.

"You're a sick person bringing her here," my father's friend said, getting in my mother's face, "You're a very sick person."

I had always despised this friend. My father had known him since childhood. He owned a business and lived large. My father was a longshoreman, a union man. He was enamored of his friend's lifestyle and tried his best to emulate it. One time, the man came over to our house in a tacky red sports car, parked in my mother's spot in the driveway and had to tell me about the "little car"—a Corvette—which he had just purchased for his daughter. "What did your father get you?" he asked. He knew I drove an old Chevy Cavalier station wagon. My father sat there looking at his callused hands, silent.

My father came around to my side of the car. I locked the door and shrank down further in my seat. "Did she make you come here? Huh, did the crazy lady make you come here?" my father peered into the passenger window. I was silent and looked down as he knocked on the window, trying to get my attention.

My mother got back in the car and sped all the way home, my father following us in the Civic.

As soon as my mother roared up the driveway, I ran inside, grabbed my bag and donned my polyester uniform. I had never been so happy to go to work at Rickels Home Center. I fled toward the station wagon. Coco, our dog, sensing the oncoming insanity, ran out after me. Normally, when freed, the dog ran down the street, and went digging in garbage cans. Then we'd have to drive through the development, shouting out the name of his favorite food: "Cheese! Coco, we have cheese!" Neither garbage cans nor the promise of cheese could sway him from the spectacle of my parents. He stood frozen, ears at attention.

My mother was in front of the driveway, my father was across the street, shaking his Members Only jacket in his fist.

"Is this the way you're gonna be? Huh?" my father taunted. He had that familiar look, the look that preceded the crazy.

"Fuck you," my mother said in deep Staten Island.

"No, fuck you," my father creatively replied.

"Fuck me?" My mother asked, her voice taking on the tone of a Mafia don.

"Yeah, fuck you."

My parents inched closer to each other. A few neighbors watched from down the street.

My father shoved my mother. Hard.

"You fucking son of a bitch," my mother yelled.

Coco barked. He had always hated fighting, frequently attempting to break up the family quarrels, but he did not approach them. He stood on the front lawn, with one paw pointing in the direction of my parents alternating between a whimper and a growl, unsure of what to do. It was as if the dog had read my mind; I felt exactly the same way. I took him by the collar and got into my station wagon. I sat in the driver's seat, the dog got in the back. The Bart Simpson bumper sticker was still stuck to the glove compartment. This girl I knew, who I drove to an abortion clinic, gave me the sticker in return. The corners curled upwards, folding in upon themselves. *Don't have a cow man.*

Many of my peers were dealing with their own relationships. I had never been with anyone outside of a few fleeting one-night stands with boys who wouldn't speak to me afterward. There I was, after my first year at an elite university, sitting in the place I thought I had escaped, in my polyester uniform, on my way to a job I never thought I'd have to do again, watching as my parents screamed expletives at each other in the middle of the street. My mother now demanded details of my father's extramarital sex life.

I put the key in the ignition and started the engine. I looked hard at my parents, who were only about ten feet away from me, standing directly in front of the car. They absolutely despised each other yet they could not get divorced. There was always some reason why they couldn't: money, the Catholic Church, their general inability to move forward, always some excuse to stay together. I was convinced that they thrived on misery and were set on making me their fellow wallower. I wanted out.

I realized I could easily take out all three of us by shifting the car from park to drive and setting my foot on the accelerator. Instead, I banged my head against the steering wheel. Coco whimpered more desperately from the backseat, he leaned forward and

I felt his wet nose by my ear. My uniform top was dotted with tears.

When I looked up, my mother was also crying. She turned and made her way back up the driveway. She definitely did not deserve this, but I knew from experience that she was not going to do anything to change the situation. My father looked at me from across the street and shook his head; I couldn't tell if he was ashamed of me or him or the whole situation.

After I got my acceptance letter from NYU the year before, I was sitting at the dinner table with my parents, which I usually avoided, but I felt a bit celebratory that night. Even my mother, who somewhat regretted her lack of higher education, seemed pleased with the news and smiled as she spooned pasta onto our dishes. She asked my father, "Aren't you going to congratulate your daughter? She just got into NYU."

My mother's question prompted the kind of instantaneous and uncalled for violent response my father was known for; the way the alcoholic father in a TV movie goes crazy after drinking, my father would go crazy without any substances at all. He lifted up his dinner plate and hit me on the head, "you want to go to college? Look at you, you're as fat as a house!"

"That was completely uncalled for," my mother said in a typically ineffectual plea.

The plate shattered. I don't know if it was from the impact with my head or from slamming into the wall behind me. But in a second of shocked delirium, I was surprised that it broke: I was pretty sure it was a Correlle plate and had grown up thinking they were unbreakable.

When I finally stood, ziti cascading off of me, I felt eight feet tall, indestructible, with the urge to destroy my father. I picked up the giant serving bowl of macaroni and dumped it on his head, then smacked him with the serving spoon. From somewhere, my voice screamed, in a tone I was sure hadn't before come from me, "*YOU DON'T HIT ME! YOU DON'T HIT ME ANYMORE!*"

I got in the Chevy Cavalier and just drove, blasting the classic rock station, screaming along with Robert Plant to "The Immigrant Song," chunks of tomato sauce still clinging to my hair. When I returned to the house, I did not look at or speak to my father for a month after this. He would never hit me again.

For those weeks, my father looked pained, his eyes perpetually downcast, like our dog when he knew he'd done something wrong. One day I came home to find an article from *The Star-Ledger* taped to my bedroom door. The article was about acclaimed children's author Paula Danziger and her work with middle schoolers. My father had written NYU ALL THE WAY atop the article in block letters, and he had made a box around a paragraph in which Danziger is quoted about the importance of character development. He was not a book reader and he had no idea who Paula Danziger was, or that I had enjoyed her books when I was younger, but beneath this, he'd written, VERY IMPORTANT. NYU ALL THE WAY. GOOD LUCK. LOVE DAD.

That summer afternoon I stared at my father as he stood between our cars, looking like he wanted to explain something to me, but couldn't find the words.

He turned and silently climbed into his not-good-enough red Civic, clutching his beloved fashion relic in his hands.

3

We Are Family

THE TASTEFUL SMATTERING OF EYE SHADOW GLITTERED, complimenting the fuchsia sequined headband nestled in a shiny, floppy highlighted bob. The t-shirt was Divine, as in the actor in the John Waters film *Desperate Living*. Baggy jeans, awkward on such long legs, and beat up suede sneakers clashed with the shiny upper body. “Hello, darlings,” said the lanky figure posing in our doorway.

Intriguing, I thought.

Cathy, my new roommate, a junior, introduced him as Keith, a friend from her freshman year, who lived down the hall.

When I held out my hand, he kissed it. While I wasn’t so keen on the poster of Cathy’s crush, Data, the android from *Star Trek: The Next Generation*, staring at me while as I slept, I was elated to be back at school. There weren’t too many hand-kissing men wearing shimmery eye shadow in suburban New Jersey.

"Nice t-shirt," I said to Keith. "I love John Waters." I'd seen his film *Hairspray*. It was the first time I'd seen a happy, confident fat girl on celluloid, and a monumental event in my life.

"Ah," Keith said with a grin. "A girl after my own heart. We should totally date, except I'm gay."

"Really?" I asked sarcastically, "I would have never known."

"We can still be friends, though. If you promise to keep your hands to yourself," he said with a laugh.

"I'll try my best," I said, annoyed he'd brought up the "desperate fat girl falling for a gay guy," trope. But, when it seems you've found the human unicorn you've been searching for for years, you tend to overlook such things.

Besides our John Waters mania, we soon found out we shared an affinity for black cherry soda, Manic Panic hair dye and Madonna's *Truth or Dare* documentary, which we watched on a loop, while saturating our hair in vegetable dye and continuously quoting Ms. M's simple but notable lines: "the fascist state of Toronto," "put me on their fucking frequency," or "do my eyebrows."

We were fellow New Jersey escapees striving to be big city art geeks. Keith was an aspiring drag queen who drew style inspiration from late '80s Jersey girls. I was a wannabe performance artist drawing on my general distaste for Jersey. Neither of us had fallen far from the tree of alienated suburban adolescence.

I'd lost about twenty pounds between high school graduation and the beginning of sophomore year, but thanks to the combination of late-night dancing in gay bars with Keith, early morning walks home for lack of cab fare, and a limited food budget, I shed another forty pounds. By the time spring arrived, I had purchased my first pair of shorts in years from the sale rack at The Limited and uncovered an old pair of black jeans I had outgrown in the sixth grade which, at 19, fit to perfection.

Keith and I began crashing art parties, taking advantage of the open bars and free crudités. One time, Keith found out about a fancy loft party for a new glossy gay magazine called *OUT*. He interned at a small film production company and his boss, a well-respected underground filmmaker, had been invited to the party, but couldn't make it. Keith, in boy clothes, pretended to be the filmmaker and I pretended to be a well-known lesbian filmmaker.

"Uh, yeah," the door guy, said, incredulous, as we told him our "names." But, he let us in.

I don't think I'd ever been inside a SoHo loft before and I was impressed by its size as well as the sparse, yet elegant, adult décor. Our fellow partiers were mostly affluent looking (although most people looked affluent to us at the time) white men, at least a decade older than we were. Occasionally someone smiled in our direction, but no one approached. Soon, we piled cheese cubes onto tiny paper plates—we were the only ones at the snack table—and awkwardly took up space by the bar, Keith started gasping for breath, staring into a corner of the room.

"What's wrong?" I asked.

Keith didn't answer, but continued to gasp. I followed his glance and joined him in gasping.

My cheese cubes shook, a rush of adrenaline sped through my body. Keith and I looked at each other, silently screaming, "*Holy shit, that's John Waters!*"

We moved away from the bar and retreated to the opposite side of the loft.

"We have to talk to him," I said. "Or else we'll be complete losers."

We decided to stand near him, ready to approach when the group of people around him scattered. After a while, their conversation ended, and we looked up from our plates and drained our wine glasses. Together, we approached our artistic hero and revealed our true identities as geeky NYU students and fans of his work. We explained how we got into the party, how we crashed such parties often, how we were typically the only ones eating the crudités.

With an amused smile on his face, he told us a bit about his own brief time at NYU film school. He had lived in the same dorm that I had my freshman year. He dropped out shortly after to actually make films.

"This is my producer, Pat," John Waters said, introducing a smiling blond woman. "Pat, these are the most interesting people at the party," he said in a way that convinced me he wasn't kidding.

"I can tell," she said, approvingly.

My body was stiff with glee, and next to me, Keith contained his trembling. We decided to make a graceful exit.

"So nice to meet you both," I said, currently the more verbal geek.

"Nice to meet you both too," they each said.

Filled with cheese and still glowing from our fantasy conversation, we decided to leave the party a few minutes later.

As we exited, Pat walked by, "have a great night kids," she said. And we did.

That summer, between my sophomore and junior years, I rented the walk-in closet of an upscale apartment in an exclusive building in the West Village. I borrowed a friend's futon, which seemed to weigh a thousand pounds. I trussed and moved the mattress from her apartment just a few blocks away. This took a while and no matter how hard I tried, I couldn't keep parts of it off the ground. When I finally rolled the partially tar-stained mattress, sparkly with street, into the building, past the suspicious doormen, through the palatial lobby, onto the elevator and up to the apartment, I realized it took up the entire closet floor, the sides lining up along the walls, like a giant hot dog bun. I didn't own any sheets, but I could access the central AC if I kept the closet door open, the cable TV was always on in the den and the house bong was three feet tall with a perpetually full bowl. These amenities would negate the fact that I would be spending the summer sleeping as a human frankfurter.

I had a pair of Dr. Martens oxblood boots held together with electrical tape, a milk crate brimming with books on French existentialism and a cardboard box containing a half dozen articles of clothing that didn't quite fit me anymore. I could have acquired hangers for my outsized pants and t-shirts, but hangers would signify a sense of permanence that, at age 19,I was not ready to embrace.

There were three "real" bedrooms in the apartment, each occupied by wealthier NYU classmates. My roommates included Holly, an intern at an art gallery who was fully endowed by her parents. Jon, who occupied the loft area of the apartment, was a full-time TV intern who also never had to worry about lunch money. And Jean, who worked as a phone sex operator, but also has a bit of a trust fund air about her.

The closet rental worked for everyone involved. I had a place to sleep and my roommates had an extra $275 a month to spend on cocaine.

Mornings, I would pull on a pair of jeans, dig up that day's t-shirt, lace up my Dr. Martens and leave the closet. My roommates kept a gallon of strong iced coffee in the fridge at all times.

I would help myself to a mug of iced coffee and drink it at the kitchen island, as I swallowed my birth control pill. I had been on the Pill, mainly for cramps, since I was seventeen. Luckily, was able to get the pills for $5 a pack at the University clinic and had stocked up for the summer. I thought of my daily coffee/Pill combo as my continental breakfast. One morning, as I enjoyed my hormones and caffeine, Jon stood nearby adding milk to his tall glass of coffee.

"I can't believe you just took a birth control pill in front of me," he said.

"Why?"

"You're not supposed to do that in front of guys," he scolded. "It's supposed to be a secret."

I felt like popping another one just to piss him off, but I refrained.

On the elevator down, I stood among the real residents in their corporate wear, I imagined they were trying to figure out what family I worked for as a nanny, or perhaps they thought I was one of their neighbor's downwardly mobile daughters just back from rich kid detox.

Keith lived nearby in a tiny studio he shared with Amy, a slightly unhinged woman, Amy's decidedly unhinged mother, and their two unfixed, non-housebroken cats, who spent most of the day humping and peeing on everything. Keith had just graduated and was broke, which explained the horrible living situation. Occasionally, I spent an evening in their litter box of an apartment, listening to Amy's diatribes outlining her frighteningly detailed castration fantasies and her mother's rants about her "nightmare of a faggot ex-husband," as the aptly named Puddles the cat peed on my jeans.

Keith and I spent a lot of time at my place, pairing Juicy Juice with cheap plastic jug vodka, as my female roommates drank slightly more mature gin and tonics and did lines of cocaine. They were generous with their stash, and determined to get me to try it, but I had no interest. Cocaine seemed to be for others: the kind of girls who interned at art galleries, dated older men who wore suits and who made chocolate truffles as a hobby. My resistance seemed to annoy them and they jokingly "peer pressured" me to do blow on a daily basis. I didn't give in, but I did take advantage of the perpetually full bowl on their three foot bong.

After our fill of bottom-shelf beverage and free bong hits, Keith and I would head over to the East

Village to hit up the usual places: Dick's Bar on 12th St. and 2nd Ave.; Wonder Bar on 6th Street between avenues A & B; and finally to Crow Bar on 10th St. and Avenue B, where we would take up a portion of the back room, typically hanging with some other gay guys, and laugh/crying about something. I might flash my boobs, and Keith might cackle, "Oh my god, sometimes I forget you have tits." The boys in turn, might show me their stuff, which would prompt the older guy who had been lurking in the corner to scoot closer. He wore overalls and a t-shirt, and had glasses and thinning hair. He must have been at least 30, maybe even 35! The guys would button up and sit down. The elder would offer to buy us free drinks.

The summer I lived in the closet, I also came out of the closet, at least to myself. Keith had been coaxing me for while. "You would make such a great dyke!" he would say, often in public and apropos of nothing. I was not confused by my attraction to women, but I was baffled about how to proceed. Lesbians seemed so scary and intimidating, just a little too cool. It was safer to just hang with my gay brothers, but I decided to go to my first lesbian bar that summer.

"Come *on*, I'm always going to gay bars with you!" I argued with my nelly chosen siblings.

"Yes, but gay bars are actually fun," they retorted.

Eventually, Keith and the boys accompanied me to Crazy Nanny's on Seventh Avenue South. I led the pack entering the bar and as soon as I entered, proudly wearing my shorts from The Limited, I felt exposed, like one of those dreams where you show up at school and you're naked in front of your entire class. The women in the bar were older, like over 30, and they were all looking at me like I was a freak. Or at least I thought they were. I tried to turn around, but the boys wouldn't budge. Instead they pushed me forward.

"This will hurt us more than it hurts you," one of them said. I sat huddled in the corner with the guys, afraid to talk to anyone. We stayed for one drink and quickly headed out to go dancing at Crow Bar.

By the end of the summer Keith and I moved to the East Village, me to a dorm on East 7th Street and Keith to an apartment off Avenue B.

He bedazzled a housedress from Woolworth's, bought a curly, auburn wig and a pair of cheap high heels. I donated an outsized bra and panty set and my dead aunt's tacky costume jewelry to the drag cause and "Eva" was born. Over seven feet of fabulous, Eva had legs up to here and big, fluffy, fake Jerseyfied hair. I accompanied Keith to his drag shows, cheering from the sidelines and often holding Eva's purse. This may seem like a demeaning task, but you'd be amazed at the places you can go with a 7-foot-tall drag queen. Soon we flirted our way into clubs, the admission typically paid for by Keith's towering drag presence.

Keith gave me a copy of Valerie Solanis's *The SCUM Manifesto* and my first vibrator for my 20th birthday in September, saying these were necessities for today's young woman. I put both to good use. The Solanis book piqued my interest and acted as a springboard for my further radical feminist study. My job at the NYU Book Center came to good use as well. During breaks and down time, I would pull up a stool to the Women's Studies section and read all I could about patriarchy, pro- and anti-pornography feminism, and reproductive rights. This independent study into the various avenues of female oppression was a mind-blowing experience and explained so much about my life as a girl. I was particularly intrigued by a tome I came across, featuring many uncompromising women performance artists, which completely broke open my worldview. *Angry Women*, which included a series of interviews with some cutting edge women artists and thinkers like Karen Finley and bell hooks. I found their visions and dedication to their work inspiring.

Soon, I started to write narrative prose poems depicting the oppression I felt as a fat teenage girl in the suburbs. I read one of my pieces, "Fat Girls Don't Wear Spandex," an angry free-form rant for a class assignment and managed to scare some of my more mainstream-focused classmates. I made a pledge to myself that I would start to put my work on stage.

Keith and I continued making our fruity homemade cocktail concoctions, this time hanging out most weekends in Keith's "bedroom," which was actually the hallway between the living room, (his socially backwards roommate's room), and the bathroom. The roommate would often settle in for the night with a bowl of generic macaroni and cheese, listening to an endless loop of *Blondie's Greatest Hits* on his cassette Walkman. After closing the beaded curtain that separated us from Mac & Cheese man, the hallway became a chamber of transformative delights as Keith painted and poured himself into Eva, who had recently acquired a hot leopard ensemble, then added glitter to my red lipstick to the tune of '70s disco legends singing about survival and cakes in the rain.

Around midnight, buzzed from the vodka and pumped up from the wisdom of the divas, we headed the few blocks over to our favorite club, Crow Bar, where we took up residence near the back, and where Eva greeted both friends and admirers. Watching my geeky film school friend, also from New Jersey, fit into the role of a bitchy yet classy hostess, taught me that transformation was possible. I embarked on my own.

I'd been sleeping with Eric, a guy from school, since sophomore year. He was non-threatening, he shared his weed with me, and his job at Two Boots pizza made me privy to lots of tasty leftovers. He would stop by my dorm once in a while, still wearing his tomato-stained apron and holding a pizza box. The first time, the dorm guard was surprised that I signed him in, rather than just handing over a wad of bills in exchange for the pizza.

But, like two porno movie tropes passing in the night, the college girl and the pizza delivery guy made their way upstairs. My roommates liked it when he came over, as we shared the picked-over pizza products with them. "Are you fucking Eric tonight?" they would ask. "I'm in the mood for Stromboli." And free, slightly congealed Stromboli they would get.

Although Eric provided me with the delightfully unholy trinity of marijuana, pizza and sex (and occasionally, beer), this was no great romance. Except for the aforementioned vices, we didn't have much in common, and couldn't really carry on a conversation when we weren't stoned out of our minds, but we continued this pattern for most of the year. And Keith continued in his quest to make me a dyke."You need to find yourself a good woman. What has the pizza man done for you lately?"

I tried asking girls out, but got tongue-tied, or was misunderstood, or plain shot down. I once handed a quirky art chick I had crush on a flyer for a gallery show I wanted to see. *10,000 Years of Penis Envy* it read on fluorescent pink paper.

"What's this?"

"A flyer for a show featuring a collection of dildos decorated by various female artists. Sounds pretty cool."

"Yeah. Totally," she said. "I might go."

"Great. Would you like to go together?"

"No, not really. Sorry." She said, handing the flyer back to me.

Discouraged, I kept up the Eric habit, while pining for a girlfriend.

I continued to write, read, work and go to school, in sort of that order. Keith found out about a poetry and video festival and we decided to collaborate on a version of "Fat Girls Don't Wear Spandex." In my long-awaited performance debut I read the poem while doing various activities—applying makeup, sweeping the floor and cooking a box of sanitary napkins in a frying pan, as one does. Too chicken to send the work out into the world with my real name, I used a pseudonym I had dreamt up in high school—Rokzan Latrine.

Exhilarated by my foray into performance art making, and inspired by Keith's drag career, I became more focused on getting my work out. The summer after sophomore year, I began attending the open poetry slams at the Nuyorican Poets Café, with the intention of reading my work. But, as soon as I rounded the corner of East 3rd Street and Avenue B, I was seized with what I would later refer to as "stage stomach," followed by a rush of excitement so intense it made the thought of getting up to read terrifying. Once, I even signed up to read with a false name, then pretended not to be there when it was called.

One night, I made a pact with myself to not chicken out. I arrived alone and paced outside the café for half an hour, before I marched to the front of the bar, where the host was writing down names for the open slam list. When he asked for my name, I blurted, to my surprise, "Cheryl B." I had never used that moniker, nor had I thought much about taking a pseudonym. In that moment, I had inadvertently reinvented myself. I didn't win the open slam that night, but I heard uncomfortable laughter at all the right times. I felt as if I had just discovered a hidden super power, an ability to make the audience simultaneously laugh, think and squirm.

Momentarily satisfied with my artistic life, and feeling smug in my familial attachment to Keith, I set my sights on getting the girlfriend.

4

The First Two

OVER THE NEXT FEW MONTHS, I CONTINUED TO DO OPEN MICS, slowly becoming more comfortable onstage, and eventually I was asked to do a Friday night Slam, which was invitation-only and a big deal. The show's theme was "Valentine Love/Hate Slam," and for the first time, in the February 1994 *New York City Poetry Calendar*, I saw my new name in print. For the slam, I wrote a love/hate poem about the state of New Jersey, the site of my teenage turmoil. The poem, "Another Brick in the Mall, Part 1," involved beer, marijuana, Burger King and cunnilingus while driving on a New Jersey highway.

So there I was in Keansburg, NJ
in the good old USA
in the house of someone whose ex-girlfriend's

brother's mechanic used to know someone who used to be a roadie for Black Sabbath,
which is why I was surrounded by the girls with the hair and the nails and the bad skin and the fluorescent orange bikinis attached to their seaside baked bodies
perchance to meet Ozzy Osborne or more likely
perchance to suck the cocks of the many local all-male band members that were in attendance
It was hard for me,
the plump and dumpy Italian chick in my "I'll see you on the Dark Side of the Moon" t-shirt and black stretch pants as I was more interested in the solution to my own suicidal tendencies than I was in any of the people in the room
I drank my fourth beer, a Budweiser, which was handed to me by a guy,
that the girl I worked with at Rickels Home Center told me was really into fat chicks,
he was a real chubby chaser
he was tall, blond and homely
and he had a beard, which in retrospect made him look like a closeted seventies leather man.
I lit my second joint of that day and took a good hit
I drove my car slowly and smokily through the Burger King drive-thru
my eyes bloodshot and my head in the clouds
the Iron Maiden leather man's head in my lap,
my Lane Bryant stretch pants on the floor
he was burping incoherently as he attempted desperately to perform cunnilingus
the girl in the BK drive-thru was appalled although she probably didn't know what the word appalled

meant,
her frosted hairs stood on end, her blue eyeliner
pooled in the corner of her eye
I felt like smearing the eyeliner down her fake red
cheeks
instead I drove off and lifted the leather man's face
out of my crotch by his hair, wishing he was a girl,
preferably Sylvia Plath
I stopped and handed the boy my Whopper and told
him to get out
He did
I drove off, I looked down and saw my pubes and
I wondered if it was legal to drive with your genitals
exposed in New Jersey
I knew it was illegal to drive barefoot
oral sex was also not legal in New Jersey
I had therefore committed two crimes
I was an oral offender
Pubic Enemy Number One
I spread my legs and fingered myself with my right
hand as I was driving with my left, the taste of beer
and French Fries in my mouth
I burp
I skid
I pass a Students Against Drunk Driving billboard
I think of Sylvia Plath and I burp again.

The week leading up to the show, I practiced nonstop. I had anxiety dreams in which Madonna, one of my idols, was a judge and absolutely hated my poems. When I arrived at the Nuyorican on the big night, with my first girlfriend and a group of college friends in tow, I spent a good amount of time in the bathroom dry-heaving. But, when I finally took the stage, I looked out at the packed house, which earlier in the evening I was sure would make me faint, and I felt calm, at home, like I belonged. I was living the dream of my shy, stuttering, former fat chick self: People wanted to hear me speak. I was finally doing "art."

That reading was the first time I felt the heady, powerful rush that only comes from connecting with an audience: a mix of flirtation and adrenaline, like a big serving of sex with a side order of drugs. I won my first Slam and left the café feeling a bit post-coital and completely energized at the same time, like the way you feel when you first fall in love.

I had found my awesome place.

The kittens arrive in the East Village past midnight. My brother Greg carries them up the five flights to my apartment in an old dog training crate. As I hold the door open for him I can hear my mother's cough from two floors below, and the scent of Kool Milds wafting upwards, a carcinogenic trumpet, announcing her arrival.

She had called a few hours earlier asking me to please take the kittens. My father didn't want them in the house anymore and he threatened an old-fashioned duffel bag kitten drowning. He was serious. He hated cats. He was the self-proclaimed King of his Castle and probably bipolar, although he would never go in for a diagnosis.

I lived in a small two-bedroom apartment with my girlfriend Pam, and Keith. Keith sleeps in a garishly decorated garret off the galley kitchen. Pam and I share a bed in the larger bedroom, where I also keep my worn-out Mac Classic perched precariously atop a file cabinet, I sit on the bed with the keyboard on my lap to type. Keith and Pam pretty much took over the décor, scattering various John Waters accoutrement throughout the apartment and placed a fluffy black gown, purportedly once worn to an awards show by Natalie Merchant in the vestibule. All this kitsch kind of drives me crazy, but it's two against one.

We eat off of a card table with folding chairs in the living room. I remove a pile of papers from the table, fold it and place it against the wall so my brother can install the feline exhibit. Our adult cats, Sabrina and Sweetie, (whom Pam and I had recently adopted in a bid to save our souring Sapphic existence), immediately circle the cage, hissing at the miniature interlopers, who reply with a chorus of tinier hisses. My mother smokes, nervous energy floating out with each exhale, flicking her ash into a bodega candle atop the TV. Most of it winds up in our haphazard collection of scattered Astroturf pieces on the floor.

"Be careful with the ash, Mom. I think that Astroturf is flammable."

"*Sorrrry,*" she exaggerates, looking down at the cracked, wood floorboards, not covered in fuzzy, green squares. "You need a nice Oriental rug in here."

"Actually, why don't you go smoke by the window? The place is starting to stink." I say.

She makes a face, but opens the window slightly and pulls up a folding chair.

"Making your mother sit on a folding chair," she says with a shake of her head, clucking her tongue. "Would you make your mother sit by the window?" She finally acknowledges Pam, who sits on the busted-up futon in her knee-length lesbian shorts unwrapping a Little Debbie snack cake, swinging her bare foot back and forth.

"If she was going to smoke, I would," Pam says, taking a bite out of her Nutty Bar.

"Where did you get your manners?" my mother asks me.

"From you, duh."

Pam smiles, my mom clucks her tongue again.

"You totally set yourself up for that one," I say.

Greg comes out of the bathroom.

"There's no sink in there," he says in a manner that suggests he's telling me something I don't know. He has a way of speaking that is both stoner clueless and art-snob condescending.

"Yeah you have to use the tub."

"You should put up a sign in there."

"Yes, I'll put one up just for you."

"Hostile," Greg says.

Pam turns on the TV to an old black & white sitcom. This is how she spends most of her days and nights, barefoot, in shorts, in front of the TV. She's mostly unemployed, working the occasional PA job, barely scraping together her part of the rent. Pam's my first girlfriend and I feel the need to take care of her even though we fight all the time. She's been particularly agreeable tonight about taking in the kittens, considering my mother typically only acknowledges her as "my friend" and my father doesn't even not know she exists. He doesn't know about my "lifestyle." But tonight we lesbians are perfect for something. We are perfect feline receptacles. Dumping them on us is less embarrassing than dropping them off at the local shelter, which I had suggested to my mother earlier in the evening. As with all the unpleasantness that stems from my father's undiagnosed mental issues, she'd rather keep it in the family.

"Dude," Greg says to Pam, extending his hand to introduce himself.

"Hey," she allows, but doesn't get off the couch.

"The TV holding up pretty good?" Our television belonged to my brother when he was in high school. He gave it to me last year, when he decided to give up all of his worldly possessions and move to a commune in New Hampshire. He didn't last long on the commune, but I got to keep the TV.

"Oh, yeah, thanks for the TV," Pam says, not moving her eyes from "The Dick Van Dyke Show."

I came out to my brother last year, during my final year of college. His response: "Lesbians are hot. " I think it was his way of saying it was cool with him, but it came out wrong.

"Cher, can you get me a glass of water?" my mother asks from her smoking throne.

I fill a glass straight from the faucet, ignoring the pitcher of filtered water in the fridge.

"New York water is still the best," she says taking a sip, between puffs of nicotine.

In the dog crate, the kittens begin to climb atop each other, forming an adorable, purring pile of caged beast. We all watch, *oohing* and *aahing*. Sabrina and Sweetie have retreated to our bed, huddled together even though they dislike each other. They remind me of my relationship with Pam.

"Oh, they're so cute!" my mother exclaims at the cage, "I wanted to keep one, but your father wouldn't let me."

My parents had already inherited the kittens' mother, Toulouse, several months earlier when my brother (who has been moving in and out of my parent's house for the last few years) asked my mom to watch the cat "for the weekend". My brother didn't believe in getting pets fixed. This was Tolouse's third litter. She was barely a year old. The previous two sets had perished due to her young age and undernourished body. He also claimed cats were hunters and needed to gather their own food. He didn't feed her too much regular cat food so Toulouse had become an adept predator, dragging half-dead birds into my mother's kitchen. Greg had named her after the painter Toulouse-Lautrec, but my mother, uneducated in art history, had adorned her with a tag that read "Taloose," and she usually calls her Lucy.

My brother pulls a box of Kitten Chow out of his messenger bag, "this is for the kittens."

"That's it? One small box for all of them?"

"It's late. That's all we had in the house."

"You need some curtains," my mother says, pointing her cigarette at the window which faces a brick wall. "People can see right in here."

"I don't have money for curtains or rugs."

"You could at least get a frilly valance or something."

"But then the people could still see in!" I counter in a mock-hysterical voice.

"I give up."

Pam yawns and stretches. This is a cue for me to tell my family to get the hell out.

"Well, thanks for the mouths to feed and for stinking up the place."

"Hey, I didn't smoke in here," my brother announces.

"Geez, I smoked out the window. Here, I'm putting it out now," my mother grinds her cigarette into the candle. "You need to get some ashtrays."

"Whatever. Look, we have to go to bed."

My mother peeks into our bedroom, where a random collection of sheets are cascading off the bed, clothes strewn across the floor. She doesn't say anything about the mess, But the pained look on her face says: *Living in sin. My daughter is living in homosexual sin.* That's like a double sin.

"Goodnight," Pam says, walking past my mother and brother to the bathroom.

"Are you throwing us out?" my mother half-whispers to me.

"It's like 2 in the morning."

Greg gets it. "Come on, Mom! We should go."

"Kicking your own mother out..."

My brother gives me a half-hug at the door. My mother leaves a big, beige lipstick stain on my cheek.

"Goodnight, um, Pam," my mother says to the bathroom door.

"Bye," Pam says in an edgy sing-song voice.

I lock the door. It's just too late to fight, I think. After a quick check on the kitten pile, which seems to be collectively asleep, I get in bed with the adult cats and pretend to sleep myself, to avoid any forthcoming wrath. I would stay on the lopsided couch, but that would definitely be asking for an argument. The sex stopped a while ago. We are now disagreeable roommates at best, but Pam is still insistent on us sleeping together, even if we aren't sleeping together.

I met Pam through Keith. They'd been friends

before Keith and I met. Pam had moved away and returned to New York the summer before my senior year of college. She and Keith became roommates, and after a bizarre courtship, she and I became girlfriends. This is what happened:

I was twenty, had never had a relationship. Up against the tile in the bathroom of a drag bar, she became The First One. Our tongues touched, cheap vodka and Hawaiian Punch buzzed between us. We formed our own planet of saliva and sweat, a devouring grind of dueling belt buckles and knee caps, the kiss, the embrace, floating...

Until a satin-fisted queen rapped on the door. "Let's go, dykes! The ladies have to piss..."

Early on, Pam told me she wasn't a nice person. She actually said, "I'm not a nice person" and we did it anyway.

Before I could trace the word "U-Haul" on her bare back, We had moved in together, shared an apartment with a drag queen and two cats. We did it covered in sequins and cat hair

She didn't like my baby doll dresses and despised my "patriarchal" shoes; She told me I was too fat to wear those pants; She was incensed by my lack of sports bras; she chastised me because she thought I cut in line at Nobody Beats the Wiz; She made me cry during board games, then laughed at me for crying; She reminded me she wasn't a nice person. We stopped doing it

She told me no one would love me like she loved me. She took down my Emily Dickinson poster and told me she hated spoken word, the other poets were flirting with me, couldn't I see that?

She buried my classic cock tapes in the closet. She told me we could only listen to women's music and we became fans of a local dyke band.

At this moment I would like to just leave, but there is the matter of the apartment. It's rent-stabilized and even though there is a heroin dealer on the first floor and no sink in the bathroom, it's a pretty cute place. I spend a lot of time fantasizing about living here alone or just with Keith or some other non-romantic roommate. Even though I found our place through a friend, Pam and I are domestic partners, something we had to do to get her on my health insurance plan at work and we are both on the lease.

I'm face down, pretending to sleep, a cat lounging on the back of my legs when Pam enters the room and lies down. I tense up, afraid she will try to put the moves on me. Instead she reaches over me to the floor and feels around, grabs something and lays back down. A series of vibrations, the bed quakes beneath her sighs, sounds that I used to find irresistible, now seem both pathetic and oppressive. I remain stiff, a numb board of a woman afraid to move as she rocks beside me. I have spent my entire 22 years struggling to get away from my parents and their screwy rendition of a marriage, only to find myself in my own supremely screwy rendition of a marriage.

We find homes for the kittens, even keep one ourselves. In a few months, Pam will convince me that Keith needs to move out, that we will be better off, stronger, closer with him gone. Not wanting to give up on my first love, I go along with this and sever ties with Keith for years.

Pam, The First One, and I finally break up, split the rent-stabilized apartment down the middle, daring each other to leave. I start seeing The Second One, the guitarist from the dyke band, who offers me rides on her motorcycle and drives me around in the band van. In a booth in a bar off the Bowery, it was hard to tell who was sitting in whose lap, whose fingers touched whose hips, whose dyed black hair was caught in the communal mouth, lost in a hard-edged whiskey swoon, guided by the bass, the beat crashing down, as we rocked into each other. It was good to be with the band.

The First One found out I was seeing The Second One, and called me a "whore." She called my mother and told her I was getting into a van with a stranger, sometimes I got on a motorcycle. My mother called me at work to check on me, fearing I had joined "some sort of mobile prostitution unit."

The First One told me I had to move out, pushed me down a flight of stairs to prove her point. I squatted on couches for weeks with the hope that she would leave.

The Second One, Jen, told me she liked to destroy people, she actually said, "I like to destroy people," and we did it anyway. Jen wanted me to move in with her, she told me her last girlfriend just waited around for her to get home, she said she wanted to put me in a human bird cage.

She cleared off a shelf for my underwear and socks, told me I could stay there whenever I needed. Early on, she gave me keys to her place, but I was too shy to use them. I waited for her in a bar with a backpack full of panties, some deodorant and toothpaste.

She arrived late, staggered over to my bar stool, her eyes were bloodshot. She smelled strange but familiar. Her kiss tasted like someone else. She burped out apologies, she didn't mean to have sex with her friend, it was all that wine she drank earlier. Her friend was passed out at her house, post-coital and there was only room in her bed for two.

The First One had accused me of eating one of her apples earlier that evening, I was now a forbidden fruit thief, unwelcome on my own couch. I spent that night at a diner with a cheese blintz, my journal and pen. And among the junkies nodding off and the elderly men having coffee with inconspicuous confidantes, the tang of ancient dried condiments in the air, I communed with Gloria Gaynor, and began work on the lesbian spoken-word version of "I Will Survive." Until my head inched toward Formica, my arm protecting a plate of cheese filling as if it were something precious I didn't want to lose.

5

Limbo

MY PARENTS DINE AT A CHINESE BUFFET IN THE WEEKS BETWEEN Thanksgiving and Christmas. My father has always taken the phrase "all you can eat" very seriously. To him, it's more of an impetus, a challenge. He does not discern between Orange Chicken and Ambrosia Salad; it all belongs on the end of his fork at the same time. My mother has already called him a pig and does not notice at first when he falls to his knees in the parking lot of Caldor after some post-buffet shopping. She walks ahead of him toward their car, smoking a cigarette.

That same Saturday, I'm with Jen when her bandmate Willy phones to ask if we would accompany her to a belated Thanksgiving dinner at her brother's house in Staten Island. We say yes and Willy picks us up in the band van, Willy's mother is already in the passenger seat, so we sit in the back. I lived on Staten Island until I was eleven and most of my extended family still live there. As we navigate the borough's curvy maze of narrow side streets, I remember riding my bike through similar terrain. The only other times I'd driven in Staten Island, I was with my parents, visiting family. It seems wrong to be there without visiting relatives, but it's also vaguely exciting. Last year, I was home for Thanksgiving. That night my father pulled me out to the garage and showed me a coffee can he kept in one of his tool cabinets.

"You see this coffee can?" he said, holding it in front of my face.

"Yes," I answered.

"There's money in here," he said, opening the can and pulling out a wad of bills. "This is money I won at the track. Whenever I win I put the money in the can. If something happens to me, you take this money. You got that? And don't tell your mother or your brother about it." With that he replaced the can and closed the cabinet door. My father knew I was frugal like him, or as my mother would say "a cheap bastard" and that I wouldn't lose the cash. I wasn't sure what he wanted me to do with the money or why he was saving it in a can but I didn't question it. I didn't think there could be that much money in there, considering it was kept in a garage that was always open.

On Staten Island at the dinner table, Jen and I are seated next to each other and across from Willy's brother's single friend. I don't think Willy is out to her family. And perhaps because of this, her brother has invited a friend, seemingly to be introduced to Jen or me as a potential love connection.

Jen is six years older than I am, 29 to my 23 and good at flirting with men. Jen holds her own, trading repartee with The Friend. Willy takes off her baseball cap, ruffles her short hair and smiles at me. She's seen this before. I originally had a huge crush on Willy, but Jen had a crush on me and she was sort of the "hot one" in the band and her desire for me made her more attractive. Jen reaches over and grabs my hand under the table, squeezes it hard. The Friend looks across the table and notices the hand-holding but that doesn't stop him from handing Jen his business card as we leave the house later on. At the door, I watch Jen put it in her back pocket. Men are always giving her their phone numbers. I find them scattered about her apartment written on the backs of deli receipts and on the insides of matchbooks.

After the trip to Staten Island, Willy drops us off at a party in the Meatpacking District and drives her mother home in the band van. The party scene is comprised of theater people; actors, directors and playwrights from the young artists lab I'm part of at a Soho theater and as such, there is an air of pretension, but I kind of like it.

Jen makes a face as we enter the loft. She hates this stuff.

"We don't have to stay long," I say apologetically before I am engulfed in a swarm of hugs and multiple repetitions of the phrase "you look amazing." Most of my colleagues are straight girls in cocktail dresses, expensive heels and well-applied eye makeup. I'm in a motorcycle jacket and the same jeans I've been wearing for three days. I'm wary of what they mean by "amazing."

Jen rolls her eyes at the display of two-sided kisses then notices a mirror covered in white powder on the coffee table. "All right," she says heading toward it. This is shaping up to be her kind of party. She sets off to pay her respects. She kneels, introducing herself to the other mirror gazers. It's 1995, and suddenly cocaine seems to be everywhere; it's at the theater parties, the poetry readings, the dyke bar. I never touched the stuff, even when I lived in the closet and my roommates were doing it, until I met Jen. Just a few months earlier, she had held a tiny spoon up to my nose and I was instantly impressed at its ability to cut the drunk in half.

The rest of the night moves very quickly. I think it's someone's birthday. There's champagne, vodka, beer. The mirror is cleared and sullied again. Jen has made friends with the gay guys sitting around the coffee table. I stand with the slim, stylish straight girls, feeling like their special dyke cousin. There's a conversation about Sam Shepard to the right of me, Chekhov to the left of me, lots of chatter about pieces and spaces and lines. By the end of the night I've had so much to drink that if I hadn't had as much coke, I would have been wasted. I've done so much coke that if I hadn't drunk so much, I would have been too high to function. My porridge is just right.

I still officially live with Pam, but I spend most nights couchsurfing or at Jen's place. I go back to my apartment every few days to refresh my supply of underwear and use my computer. Most of my phone calls are made on pay phones. Even though I have to walk around with pockets full of change, it saves me the incessant calls from my mother, who can only reach me at work. I spend a lot of time at a café on Avenue A called Limbo, since they have a phone in a semi-private area in the back. I've come to call it my office. "I'm in Limbo," I'll say to whomever I'm calling, which pretty much sums it up.

When we return to Jen's place that night after the party, her answering machine light glows an ominous red from the floor next to her futon. We are afraid to listen to the messages, knowing they are probably angry missives from each of our exes. Jen's ex calls every day, almost hourly, threatening self-mutilation or wishing that I would JUST DIE. Pam somehow found Jen's phone number, and also calls, to ask me what I am doing with that "whore." Jen hovers her motorcycle boot over the machine to press "play." I lie back on the futon, waiting for the hate to pipe through. The first message is from Pam, but her voice sounds different.

"Um, Cheryl, your mom called." There's a pause and I can hear her swallowing. "She called a few times to say your father had a heart attack." I sit up and replay the message. I still hear the phrase, "heart attack." Pam recites the details, telling me my father was taken away by helicopter. I can picture my mother, exasperated, standing at a pay phone in the hospital, going over all this with Pam, while I was having a fake Thanksgiving with someone else's family.

He's been taken to a hospital, but she didn't know which one. Then Pam said she was sorry and she said she loved me.

"Shit," Jen says, "That fucking sucks."

I sit up, reach down and play the message again. When I hear Pam say she loves me, all I can think is that it's another way for her to try to control me. Then I feel guilty for thinking something so self-centered. I wonder where my parents are, what hospital they've taken my father to. I picture him on a gurney too small for his gigantic body, his feet hanging over the end, his body spilling over the sides. Then I remember to check my personal voice mail. I pick up Jen's phone, and dial my number. There are several messages, all from my mother in various states of distress. On the last message she finally tells me the name of the hospital and that it's in Northern Jersey. She doesn't leave a phone number.

Jen pours two glasses of ginger ale, which she usually drinks with whiskey, but this time she just adds ice. I tell her the name of the hospital and Jen calls information, gets the number, dials it and hands me the phone. I ask for my father.

My mother picks up the line. She tells me he's okay, that I should come first thing in the morning. She tells me she was really disappointed, and that everyone came to the hospital: some neighbors, my mother's friends, my aunts from Staten Island.

Everyone was there, she says, everyone but her daughter. My mother ends the conversation with her old dramatic standby, "I might as well just lay down and die."

It's past midnight, but I want to go to the hospital immediately. I feel guilty I'd spent the day with someone else's family instead of by my own father's hospital bed.

"It's too bad Sarah took the band van," I say. "I feel like I should be there now."

Jen calls the hospital and gets directions. The evening's substances gave turned on me. I am no longer high; the liquor is depressing me and the cocaine reminds me of why I am a fuck-up. After the phone call, Jen gets her two motorcycle helmets. We mount her bike, and head for the car rental place. Since I am under twenty-five, Jen puts it on her credit card.

Even though I feel suddenly sober, it amazes me that after a night of partying, we are able to rent a car. Jen seems okay driving, I'm not sure if we take the Lincoln or Holland Tunnel but as the lights inside blur into one, I decide I am an incredibly horrible person. I realize that one day my mother may "just lay down and die" and there's nothing I can do about it. When we get to the hospital, I can see my mother and uncle standing outside my father's room. This is awkward; my mother doesn't want the rest of the family to know I'm gay. When she sees us, she meets me half way down the hall. She grabs me by the arm.

"I didn't expect you to come now."

"I didn't want you to lay down and die. Where's Daddy?"

"They're in the room with him."

"What did they say?"

"The heart attack was pretty severe, but they think he'll be okay."

Jen stands beside me. For some reason, she'd carried her motorcycle helmet in to the hospital. My mother introduces herself. She'd met Pam but didn't like her and was still hoping the whole "lesbian thing" was just a phase.

As we continue down the hallway, my mother pulls me aside to ask: "What are we going to tell your uncle about her?"

"I'll say she's my friend," I offer and remember Jen telling the little boys at dinner earlier that we were "special friends."

I greet my uncle, "This is uh, my friend, Jen," I almost felt like laughing. Nothing screams "Hey look at me! I'm a big dyke!" like showing up to your father's sickbed in the middle of the night with your "special friend" who is wearing motorcycle boots and carrying a helmet.

My uncle seems unfazed by this. They shake hands and began to chat. I sit next to my mother. She scratches her left elbow with the long, pearly-beige fingernails of her right hand. This is something she does when she's nervous and can't smoke. Even though her husband had just had a heart attack, she couldn't wait to light up.

The doctor comes out of my father's room. My mother stops scratching. He tells us my father had a major heart attack. They're not sure how much damage had been done, but it looked like he was doing okay so far.

My mother, my uncle and I go into my father's room, leaving Jen in the waiting area. He's half-asleep with tubes in his nose, an IV in his arm. It's hard to look at him like that. We stand silently, watching as my father breathes and shifts in his bed. He doesn't seem to notice us. After a few minutes, we decide it's time to go. We say goodbye to my uncle in the lobby.

I ride with my mother her back to her house as Jen follows us in the rental. My mother smokes non-stop during the forty-minute drive.

"How old is she?" my mother asks. She is an expert at avoiding the obvious, glossing over say, my father's public tantrums by telling me that I need some cream blush.

"Almost thirty." I answer her.

"Too old for you. Are you having sex with her too?"

"I don't ever want to have this discussion."

"It was scary to see your father like that," she says finally. "Like he just fell down and that was it. He's going to blame the Chinese food and that's going to be all my fault."

The house is already decorated in full holiday mode: lights, candy canes, snowmen. Jen pulls in behind us, parking on the street. Before we get out, my mother looks at me and says, "I want you two in separate beds. You got it?"

"Yes! Whatever."

I show Jen to my old room and explain that my mother wants us to sleep in separate beds, but that I would be in later on.

"I don't want to piss off your mom, so I'll see you in the morning," she says and closes my former bedroom door on me.

I head to my brother's room—he's asleep on the couch in the family room. On my way, my mother calls out for me. I go downstairs to the kitchen where she smokes a cigarette and drinks a cup of microwaved coffee. She's in her robe. I sit at the table with her.

"I want to know where the money is," she says without looking at me.

At first I don't know what she was talking about but then I remember the coffee can.

"I know he told you where he keeps the money," my mother said.

"What money?" I ask, innocently.

"The money from the track."

"I'm tired. I just want to go to bed." I start to get up.

"Not until you tell me where the money is."

"Look: when he gets home you can ask him where it is."

"Then you know! You know where it is and you won't tell your mother."

"Leave me alone."

"You know that money belongs to me too. You don't know what it's like to live with him."

She'd forgotten I lived there for seventeen and a half years. I knew about the daily indignations, the unprovoked violent outbursts, the physical abuse. I knew about it all—that's why I left.

"I know what it's like."

"He's worse now. And you never come home anymore."

"I came home last Thanksgiving," I point out.

"Big deal, I'm here all the time," my mother says accusingly.

"Well, you live here. I live in the city."

"Tell me where the money is."

We go out to the garage and I look through the cabinets for the coffee can. When I find it, my mother takes it from my hands, pulls out the cash and begins counting.

The wad of bills had grown substantially since the last time I saw it. As my mother counts the cash, I realize there's something fundamentally twisted about this whole scene, something distinctly "white trash." My father is in the hospital and I've allowed my mother to pillage his coffee can full of OTB winnings in the middle of the night. We are surrounded by my father's tools and his fishing equipment. His prized striped bass, long since a victim of taxidermy, watches over us with his cloudy glass eye. My mother counts out $10,000 in total. I can't believe my father would keep so much money in the garage. She puts half the money in the pocket of her robe. The rest goes back in the coffee can which she carries with her into the house.

I feel like a traitor.

I go up to my brother's old bedroom and lie on his twin bed. My brother is 20 now. Metallica posters still line his walls and a chick in a fluorescent bikini stares down at me from the ceiling.

A few hours later, we leave again for the hospital. My mother thanks Jen for driving me to New Jersey. I hug her goodbye.

"I don't like her," my mother says.

"You don't like anyone. She did drive me to New Jersey in the middle of the night. You have to give her that." I realize how sweet it was for Jen to rent a car to drive me to my father's bedside, even though she never stopped cheating on me.

"I wish you would meet a nice guy," my mother says, "Someone from around here, someone who's not going anywhere. So you can just settle down."

When we get to the hospital, my father is awake. He looks weak but is pretty coherent. I kiss him hello and sit in a chair by his bed.

"Can you fucking believe this shit?" my father asks me while my mother and brother smoke outside.

I really couldn't fucking believe it and I nod my head in agreement.

"I'm never eating Chinese food again," he tells me, "and the doctor says I have to stop smoking. That shit will kill you." He points at me, as if I'm the one on a cigarette break.

"I guess I don't have to worry about you with the smoking," he continues, "but your mother drives me up a fucking wall with her cigarettes."

I'm still wearing the same clothes from the day before and I wonder if there is cocaine residue in my nose. I feel dirty and want to go home—but which home? My parents' house is full of unwanted memories. I'm not welcome in my own apartment, the one where I still pay rent, the one I was beginning to realize I had to give up. I was living in a state of suspended animation.

When I returned to the city, I went back to my place to change clothes and stock up on socks and underwear. I grew tired of living out of my backpack, and in February I moved from the East Village apartment I shared with Pam into a sublet in Chelsea.

My father gave up smoking, but it was too late, the disease that would kill him—kidney cancer—had probably already begun to take over his body. A few months later, my father asked me over the phone if I'd "been to the can." He didn't accuse me of stealing it, but even so it pained me to lie to him since he had chosen me to entrust with his OTB winnings.

"No, I haven't been to the can," I said.

He just let out a disappointing, "okay." He never brought it up again.

That day at the hospital, we are both stuck between worlds and we didn't even know it yet.

6

The Coketail Party

IT'S A FEW DAYS AFTER CHRISTMAS IN 1996, AND MY MOTHER and I are sitting in a doctor's office. My father is outside in the waiting room. My parents met with this doctor the previous week but my mother says she doesn't understand what he's saying and she'd wanted me to come along to clarify.

"Your dad is dying," the doctor says. "He has kidney cancer, also known as renal cell cancer."

I nod. My mother had explained my father's illness to me as a kidney "problem."

"But what does that mean?" my mother asks.

"We spoke about this last week, Mrs. Burke. And I'm glad you brought your daughter along today. Your husband's cancer is too advanced now. He's a big man and after the heart attack, he just can't sustain an operation. If I put him on the table now, he'd probably expire as soon as I opened him up."

I picture my father being slapped down on a metal gurney like a big, fat dead turkey, a carving knife coming at him. I wonder if everyone gets "put on a table and opened up" or if that was just something reserved for big, brawny blue collar men.

"Do you have any questions?" The doctor asks me.

My mother still looks confused.

"How long do you think?" I ask.

"Six months," the doctor says.

In the waiting room, my father has his hands folded on his giant potbelly. He's slightly slouched, the hems of his gray corduroy pants rise to expose his white socks and the black work shoes he buys once a year at Kmart. After the doctor's office, we do what we do best: we eat at our local diner. Once we order, the three of us sit in silence. I'm 24 and in a continuing struggle for my independence, I've cut down contact with my parents in the last year. I'm also not out to my father and find it difficult to be around him. Since he was ill, I had come home for a few days for the holidays.

My father sits across from me, looking smaller than usual as he lifts a jumbo burger to his lips. He looks down at his food with resignation, leaves half of it untouched. Never before in my life have I seen him do that. Later, as he walks down the diner stairs ahead of me, still seemingly strong and healthy, a toothpick between his lips, I realize he will never be an old man.

During the next six months, I begin speaking regularly with my mother again. We speak every day about my father's condition and I go home a few weekends a month to spend time with them.

That same year, I meet a boy Chris at a soirée, what the evening's hostess refers to as a "coketail party."

He had been rude to me on the phone just the week before when he called my apartment to speak to Gina, our mutual friend who was staying at my place. I recognized his voice over the phone from an earlier brief meeting.

"Hi. Is Gina there?"

"Is this Chris? Hi, this is Cheryl."

"Is Gina there?" he persisted.

Fine. Gina was indeed there and I handed over the phone. "It's your freaky friend Chris," I said. Gina smiled and mouthed apologies.

When we meet again at the party, our teeth grinding from the coketails, I have a conversation opener.

"You were totally rude to me on the phone the other night," I say, flirtatiously punching his arm.

"Yeah, I'm sorry about that. I didn't mean it."

"Yeah, whatever," I say, executing another flirt-punch. *Why am I flirting with this guy?* I ask myself, quickly blaming the drugs.

"I was going to write you a letter, but I didn't have your address," he adds.

I'd heard Gina talk about Chris's letters. She kept a box of them from their near-romance in college. She had described them as poetic. As a performance poet, I was skeptical of most things labeled "poetic." But, I decide to give him a shot. I hand Chris my business card with my P.O. Box address and continue with the evening. After more indulgence and several speedy conversations with others, the party was coming to a close. Six of us, including Chris, stand outside, figuring out the next place to hang. It's January and freezing, so we all move in place to keep warm and give in to the jitters. I have become accustomed to all-nighters and since I live nearby, I offer up my place, but I am really only inviting Chris. In my coked-out mind, I mentally will the others to reject my offer. And they do. Chris and I head the few blocks to my house. Gina has moved out so I have the place to myself.

After we take off our coats, I wonder what the hell I'm doing. It's 5 am, a dude is sitting at my kitchen table and I'm getting out the tequila and shot glasses. (Later, Chris told me he was wondering what the hell he was doing in a lesbian's apartment at 5 am.)

I have an almost circus-freak tolerance for tequila and challenge Chris to meet me shot for shot. We keep this up for a while. In a moment of blitzed flirtation, I command him to take off his boots and stay awhile.

There is a surprising amount of passion between us, that, in my experience reaches beyond the normal heights of tequila and cocaine. After an early morning of blissful clothes-on making out, he sits across from me at the diner. I stare at my French toast suspended in a shallow creek of syrup, to avoid his dimples and baby blue eyes. What's happening to me? Am I really attracted to this guy I just made out with all morning?

When I speak to Gina that evening, I make mention of the making out, but she has apparently already been filled in.

"Did you have fun?" she asks.

"Does it bother you?" I answer her question with a question, nervous for her answer.

"Oh no," she says, "It's not like you're going to get serious or anything." She sounds tentative, like she wants me to answer: *no, of course not.*

"No, of course not!" I blurt, outraged at the thought. I mean, I'm 24 and never had a boyfriend. Why would I start so late? Not only am I a lesbian, I am a *fierce dyke poet.* I can't be running around town with some straight dude, even if he did look like a cross between River Phoenix and Keanu Reeves in *My Own Private Idaho* and would make me the envy of all my gay male friends.

Questioning my sexuality in reverse isn't the only mode of avoidance I use in handling my father's impending death. I throw myself into my work, curate a reading series, apply for the playwriting program at Juilliard, book a one-woman show for the summer, plan a spring spoken word tour, headline an event called Lesbopalooza. Drinking becomes a part-time job. I purchase a flask and keep it in my purse. When I lose the flask, I carry a Snapple Iced Tea bottle filled with tequila. Later, a friend tells me, "when I saw that Snapple bottle, I started to get worried." I find myself in a loosely organized network of pansexual partiers. Friday nights end at 1:30 Saturday afternoon. Saturday nights start after midnight on Sunday. The all-nighters become such that even my cat, Sabrina, takes action, peeing on my Payless Candies heels, the shoes I wear to go out. Chris and I continue our sloppy pursuit of each other, quietly leaving parties together. The months pass.

7

The Body

"IT'S TIME," IS ALL I CAN THINK TO SAY WHEN MY BOSS TURNS around in her chair to acknowledge me. It's early July and my mother has just called to let me know that my father is in a coma and I need to leave for New Jersey right away. Everyone in the office knows my father is dying. My co-workers watch as I stand in my boss's doorway.

When she first became my boss, we easily bonded over being gay. She even helped me find a sublet in Chelsea when I had to leave the apartment I shared with Pam. In the past few months, as I had begun dating Chris, she had turned completely cold. One time when I was five minutes late for work, she said to me, "the next time you go home with someone you pick up in a bar, make sure you bring your alarm clock." It also did not help that she reminded me of my high school guidance counselor, the one who told me I would never get into college.

"Okay," my boss said, with no hint of emotion in her voice, just like my high school guidance counselor.

My job in the textbook buying office of the NYU bookstore is secure, with benefits, which allows me to pursue my artistic endeavors. At least this is what I tell myself. A rejection letter from the playwriting program at Juilliard tells me differently. I found the letter poking out of our giant litter box the night before. I was renting a room in Williamsburg from a female junk collector who had just moved to Brooklyn from the Midwest. It seemed like she stopped at every thrift store in between and loaded up on all the crap that now adorned the apartment. Her sex life seemed to be driven more by pathology than by pleasure. She had signed up for a dating service, dated nightly and almost every time, came home with a different guy. I don't mean to judge her, but her sexual activity became my problem when, on more than one occasion, she burst into my room in the middle of the night, asking me to have a three-way with her and her man of the hour.

The Junk Collector and I both had cats. Like us, our felines did not mix well and I had to keep my cat's food and water bowls in my tiny bedroom. Then my roommate took in a pregnant stray, who promptly gave birth to six kittens. Now, months later, the kittens are still with us, even though they're way past an acceptable adoption age. The roommate does not want to get rid of them and there are cats everywhere; hanging off the crappy rattan furniture, lounging on the beaten-up beanbag chairs, practically crawling up the walls, which are covered in paint-by-numbers clowns. We have a gigantic litter box in the hallway and we dump our mail on a table above the box. The Juilliard letter protruded from below inches of litter, nestled between a monumental cat turd and a hardened pool of cat piss. The letter was postmarked a few weeks earlier and it had been forwarded from my previous address. There it was, the future of my playwriting career, what was supposed to let me leave my bookstore job, shat upon by a pack of hyperactive kittens.

At work, I walk back through our general office on my way out the door. My co-workers watch and one of them stands. I think she wants to hug me, but I can't stand the thought of being touched.

I feel like I should say something. "I'm leaving now."

One of them says, "Be strong, girl."

My mother is waiting for me in her car at the bus stop in front of the Kentucky Fried Chicken in Hazlet, New Jersey. This is the same bus stop where my parents had always picked me up from the city, and the same Kentucky Fried Chicken my father disappeared to on the night of my high school graduation after my parents got into a fight in the parking lot. My father took off in his Honda Civic after the ceremony. My mother, brother and I spent most of my graduation night looking for him. I remember my mother pulling into a parking space in front of the KFC just to turn around when we spotted my father in the headlights. He was sitting at a table by himself, a box of chicken on the tray in front of him. We didn't go in, we didn't honk the horn or make our presence known. We sat there for several moments just watching him. My fellow graduates were enjoying elaborate dinners with their families, getting wasted, having sex with their significant others while I sat in the passenger seat of my mother's car outside of a KFC, where my father spooned mashed potatoes and gravy into his mouth.

When I get into my mother's car that day in early July, she says, "he looks really bad." My mother told me she was finally contemplating divorce right before my father got sick, but instead she remained his dutiful wife, going to her secretarial job every day, leaving my father in the care of a home health aid and assuming the responsibilities at night.

When we get to the area around the hospital, the streets are thick with American flags and patriotic ribbons. Families in khaki shorts and white sneakers mill about, waiting for a fireworks display to begin. Cars are parked all over as people head down to the waterfront. There's a detour, and it takes us a few moments longer than necessary to get to the hospital. I'm convinced he'll be dead by the time I get there.

When I finally make it to my father's room, he's flanked by his sisters. My aunts move out of my way when I approach.

"Look, Cheryl's here!" one says to my father, sounding outrageously optimistic for the situation.

My father's eyes are open but blank. I don't know what to do, so I grab his hand and say hello. His gigantic hand is limp, his breath is rancid. At some point, my aunts leave, then my mother. I'm on night duty, alone with my father for the first time in years.

He's in a double room, but the other bed is empty. A nurse comes in to show me which button to press to call for help, where the visitor bathrooms are and how to adjust the air conditioner. She also tells me that he is probably going to go soon and I picture my father getting up and leaving the room. I sit on the edge of the other bed, watching him sleep. I get up frequently to pace, from the spare bed to the air conditioner panel, to fiddle with the blinds, to wash my hands. I get out my notebook and try to finish a poem. Instead, I hold the notebook open on my lap and stare into space until it slides onto the floor. This setup is not so different from our usual interactions, the two of us sitting separately, with little to say. It might even be less awkward. He looks diminished, like a large tree that has been cut down. When I lean over his bed, I notice the creases in his face, lines formed from years of working in the sun. I have never looked at him so closely, and it's like studying a familiar specimen, something that has been around all of your life, but you never paid it any attention.

I know I was supposed to spend this last night with my father telling him the things he didn't know about me, like a confessional. In my mind it would go something like this:

Forgive me father, you don't know this about me, but I'm a lesbian and I am currently mainly sleeping with a man and occasionally still sleeping with women. I am, as you put it when I was a kid, "doing my thing."

I can hold my beer just like you. Hard liquor is another story, as you know since you couldn't really handle it either, but that hasn't stopped me from drinking it flask by flask. I didn't appreciate that time you hit me in public when I was sixteen and you didn't have to kick me up the stairs when I was four and I wished you'd come to see me off when I left for college.

Do you remember the trip to the water park when I was ten? You went down the giant waterslide before me and you thought it would be funny to hold on to the sides of the slide and surprise me as the water traveled around you. Your head was thrown back in laughter. You were hooting and splashing about in the shallow stream, as I rounded a corner of the slide, head first on my mat. You didn't move even when I screamed that I was going to crash into you. Just as we were about to make contact you let go of the sides, the top of my head hit the back of yours, hard. I held on to your shoulders and we traveled down the rest of the slide together. After making your gigantic splash in the wading pool, you looked happier than ever. I didn't mention that my head hurt.

"That was something else!" you said, looking down at me with an enthusiasm you usually only reserved for Elvis Presley, "let's do it again!"

I could have told him all of this, but it remained in my head and the hours passed.

My father lived through July 4th with shifts of people—aunts and uncles, friends, cousins, neighbors—coming in and out to visit.

It happened the next day. My brother had been in the room with him as a group of us sat in the waiting area. "He has to make peace with his father," my parents' friend had said. If I knew our family, my brother was doing the same thing I did the other night; the internal monologue. So I decided I could go in, too. I closed and locked the door behind me and we both stood there, waiting for my father to die. His breathing slowed, then became unsteady, as if he had been waiting to be alone with us. I watched my brother watching him. Greg looked terrified. I watched him touch my father's arm. "It's okay," he said.

They'd had a notoriously bad relationship, which had escalated after I left for college. My mother called me one day at my dorm during my junior year to tell me that my brother and father were in the family room menacing each other with golf clubs. The clubs were hand-me-downs and one of my father's favorite possessions. I told my mother to hang up and call the police; there was nothing I could do about it from Manhattan. I could hear my father and brother screaming and my mother gasping into the phone. I heard my father call my brother a "scumbag." My roommate walked by with a concerned, questioning look on her face. "My mother," I mouthed. She shrugged as if to say "oh, okay," but still looked wary. She'd been privy to my mother's telephone madness before. I listened to my mother sighing and sobbing as my father and brother continued to scream in the background. I heard something break. "That's it," I heard my father yell. I heard a door slam. I heard my brother shout, "I can't fucking take this place anymore." Apparently, it was over. "See what I have to live with?" my mother had asked. The edge in her voice suggested that I should have an answer for her.

I have never witnessed death before and am held captive by its beauty, unable to move for several minutes after he stops breathing. My brother hugs me fiercely and I can't remember us ever having hugged before.

I'm ambling down the hallway before I even realize that I had left the room. I don't know where my brother is but my aunts pass me in the hall. One of them reaches out to touch me, but I keep walking. I remember passing another room with a woman standing in the doorway. I note her shoes: red, shiny, pointy and not really suitable for summer. My mother passes me on the way to my father's room, we do not acknowledge each other.

I find a pay phone and whip out a calling card. Of all the numbers I have memorized, the friends I could call who are waiting to hear news about my father, I choose to dial my own number. Not the home answering machine that I share with The Junk Collector, but the disembodied voicemail box I pay seven dollars a month for, the one I use for my "art."

"Hello," I hear myself say, "This is Cheryl."

I have twelve messages, but I don't check any of them. I hang up and dial myself again. At that moment, I just want to hear my own voice tell me who I am.

"I'd like to buy a family plot," my mother said when presented with the options for burying my father. My brother and I were sitting on either side at the funeral home, and quickly turned our heads to look at her. She stared straight ahead, her body stiff with resolve. She had that hurt, yet determined look in her eyes. A look that pleads "why are you doing this to me?" and cautions "how dare you?" at the same time. Her mother had the same look—both needy and controlling—a look I had observed since childhood, was common among many Italian-American women. I wondered if I too would someday acquire it.

The undertaker, a stocky Italian guy whom I'd already nicknamed Cannoli, because his skin was the same pasty white as ricotta cheese, cleared his throat. He spoke, using large, flourishing hand gestures.

"But Mrs. Burke, your children are still very young," Cannoli said, "They may want to be buried with their own families someday."

My mother shook her head. "No," was all she said.

We were in the office of the funeral parlor and the air was tinged with the overwhelmingly sick smell of too many fresh flowers.

"You have to think rationally here. Your children are still very young," Cannoli repeated. He had already sold my mother the most expensive coffin, stating something like, "it will keep him fresher longer." A purchase so outlandish, that if my father, a man who enjoyed eating lunch at K-mart, were alive and present, it would have driven him into a semi-psychotic rage.

"I want the family plot," my mother said as if that was that.

Speechless, my brother and I looked at each other.

"Because we're a family," she added, staring straight ahead.

My mother turned to give me The Look again, followed by pursed lips and a defeated sigh; this was the worst combination. My mother let out another sigh, this one far less emphatic. "I give up. I just give up," she said. Her usual saying would have been, "I might as well just lay down and die," but that must have seemed inappropriate to the situation, so she used an alternate. She was dressed in black, just as her mother was after my grandfather died. Unlike my grandmother, who wore black whenever she left the house for the four years she outlived my grandfather, my mother would only keep this up until my father was buried. My mother shook her head. I imagined her holding a set of Rosary beads, a tiny, fragile old Italian lady determined to share her eternal resting place with her children. As the eldest child, I decided to put this idea to rest.

"Well, I think," I began.

Cannoli cut me off, "Mr. Burke what should we do?"

Mr. Burke? My brother and I both turned our heads in surprise. Where was Mr. Burke? Had our dead father just walked in?

"Mr. Burke," Cannoli said again, this time looking straight at my brother, "What would you like to do?"

In that brief moment my brother had risen through the ranks from irresponsible son to man of the house. Greg was 22, perpetually unemployed, a crasher of cars, destroyer of sneakers, loser of winter jackets, player of bongos, my father's opposite. The freshly anointed Mr. Burke, for all of his coolness, was still a mama's boy.

He studied his hands, "I don't know," he said, and looked at my mother who still stared straight ahead.

"We'll take the double. For me and my husband only," my mother said in a manner that was meant for me and brother to feel as if we'd be missing out on something.

"That's an excellent choice," Cannoli jotted it down on a notepad as if he were a wine steward taking her order. "Now that we've figured that out. We'll get to work on him."

"Is he here yet?" my mother asked.

"Yes, we just got him in this morning, he's downstairs. He's in pretty bad shape. but that's typical of that type of cancer. But, he'll be ready for the wake tomorrow."

"I brought his suit," my mother said, motioning to a garment bag draped over the side of a black leather couch. "I hope it still fits. He lost so much weight being sick."

My father was not a suit type of guy. And my brother and I had suggested he be buried in his beloved Members Only jacket. That idea was quickly shot down with The Look.

"Now let's get to work on the obituary!" Cannoli sounded a little too enthusiastic about this. He dabbed his forehead with a handkerchief, which was embroidered with his initials. He had a pinky ring.

"Education?" Cannoli asked.

"He was against it," I joked remembering his rails against higher education.

"He attended New Dorp High School," my mother said.

The newly-crowned Mr. Burke put in his two cents, "yeah, for like two weeks."

Cannoli cleared his throat, "We'll just say he graduated. It sounds nicer."

"Military service?" No.

"Siblings?" Two sisters, one brother. Parents deceased.

"Children, just you two?" he asked my brother, who wasn't paying attention.

"Yes, just us," I answer, "Cheryl and Greg."

"Cheryl with an S?" he asked my brother again.

"And he worked on the docks?" Yes.

"For how long?" Forty years. This was followed by a brief silence.

"Well, I think that's it. He'll be laid out tomorrow starting at 11. We let the family in at 10 for a private viewing."

My mother grabbed hold of my brother's arm as she walked out of the office. Her black clothing and hunched presence made her seem even smaller than her five feet.

I followed them half way out the door, when Cannoli suddenly tapped me on the shoulder. "Cheryl," he said, "two more things for the obit: do you still use your maiden name?" Then he asked me if my father had any grandchildren.

This funeral parlor was a few blocks from where we used to live on Staten Island. I remember riding past on my bike when I was a kid, and stopping to pick apart discarded floral displays on the side of the building. As we left the funeral home that day, even though I was now twenty-four, I looked for fallen flowers.

My mother held on to my brother's arm as we walked to the car. The new Mr. Burke drove us back to our house in New Jersey. My mother sat in the front passenger seat, I sat in the back. Ever since my father was diagnosed with cancer in January, I'd been having extensive memories of things I'd practically forgotten. That day in the car, all I could think about was the fact that my mother had never trusted my driving.

My father taught me how to drive in the Sheraton parking lot when I was seventeen. We would come back from practicing K-turns and my mother would ask, "how bad was she?" My father, no stranger to putting me down himself would say, "She did good. Not a problem."

My father's reassurance was not enough for my mother, who, even after I passed my driving test, did not trust me to operate a motor vehicle. When she was in the car with me, she would hysterically shout directions and slam on the imaginary passenger side brake. One particularly harrowing afternoon I found myself driving my mother and Mrs. Goumba around on a Saturday afternoon during the Spring of my senior year of high school. Mrs. Goumba, who I considered an enemy because she told my parents things like, "You don't send a girl to college! Especially a fat girl, she's never going to find a husband there!" had lobbied for me to drive that day which was the only reason I was at the wheel.

I'd had my license for a few months and it did nothing for my confidence that my personal nemesis had more faith in my driving abilities than my own mother. We stopped at a gas station to fill the tank. My mother reminded me to put the car in park after I had already done so and to cut the engine while my hand was still on the key in the ignition. After getting the gas, my mother reminded me to start the car again and put it into D for Drive. I watched the Goumba's wife roll her eyes in the rearview mirror and we exchanged conspiratorial glances. "Keep your eyes on the road!" my mother said.

"Let the kid drive Phyllis!" Mrs. Goumba chided from the backseat.

"Now, slowly, slowly pull over to the opening."

It was a sunny Saturday afternoon in New Jersey and the highway was a blur with cars darting from shopping center to shopping center. My mother's foot was held firmly on the imaginary brake pedal as I attempted to inch into the traffic. With each tick forward, my mother gasped and closed her eyes until the stream of cars finally slowed enough and I was half-way on to highway, completely ready to merge. That's when she yelled, "stop!" and grabbed my right arm.

"Get out, let me drive!" my mother screamed, unfastening her seat belt, and leaving the car. The car was jutting out onto the highway, far enough to interrupt but not join in the flow of traffic. The other cars swerved around us, their drivers throwing nasty looks in our direction. My mother was so afraid to let me merge, she was willing to risk the ire of dozens of angry Jersey drivers.

"For Chrissakes Phyllis, what's wrong with you!" her friend yelled from the backseat. My mother came around to my side of the car and knocked on my window, motioning for me to get out. I refused. I locked my door, then locked the passenger side door.

My mother's friend laughed in the backseat as my mother's many-jeweled hand came knocking on the window. The charm on her giant charm bracelet clanked on the glass, a cigarette dangled from her lips. I pointed at the empty passenger seat, then pointed at her and motioned for her to get back in the car and sit down. She shook her head and pointed at me, motioning for me to get out. I shook my head. My mother's friend continued to crack up. "I'm sorry, but your mother is crazy!" Mrs. Goumba laughed harder and for once, as I watched my mother's long pearly-beige fingernail tapping on my window, I had to agree with her. My mother, noticing her friend's laughter, made her "why are you doing this to me?" face. She then let loose with a string of expletives, which I could not completely hear since the window was closed and the traffic kept coming but I could read her lips.

"You fucking son of a bitch," she said, taking a long drag off her cigarette and coming around to the passenger side. I unlocked the door and she climbed back in, "you're going to give me a heart attack, I swear."

I successfully pulled out onto the highway and I merged. "You know what Phyllis?" Mrs. Goumba said."You've turned into your mother." As family legend had it, my grandmother would not talk to my grandfather for weeks after he taught my mother to drive at 21, and refused to get into the car with her, until years later when she had to rely on my mother for transportation to and from her doctor's appointments. And, so, the cycle continued.

Years later, my partners would find the perfect word to call me during my fleeting moments of irrationality, insecurity and insanity. The one word that would stop me in my tracks and cut me to the core; they would call me "Phyllis."

The young Mr. Burke got us safely back to our house in New Jersey and the minute we arrived, I wanted to leave. Since my clothes were stuck in my closet in Brooklyn, and all I had taken with me to New Jersey was my emergency backpack from work, I decided I had to go shopping for proper funeral wear. I casually grabbed my mother's car keys and announced, "I'm going to Mandee's."

My mother threw herself in front of the door. "I'm coming with you," she said, "You never drive any more, you might get in an accident." My mother gave my brother her credit card and he took my father's car to go buy a suit. My mother and I climbed into her car, "we're going to Macy's, not Mandee's," she announced starting the car. "It's your father's funeral for Chrissakes, you don't go to Mandee's."

Macy's was in the mall. I was really not in the mood for the mall, but I found myself perusing the sale racks nonetheless. I picked out two pairs of black slacks and a few light sweaters. My mother looked over my choices and said, "you need to get a dress for the burial." I'm not much of a dress wearer so I picked out the cheapest frock I could find, a black-and-white houndstooth mini-dress with a matching black half-cardigan. It would do. In the shoe department, I picked out a pair of black heels to wear with the dress. I've always liked putting cheap outfits together for poetry shows and have chosen to view my appearance at my father's wake and funeral as a performance of sorts; Return of the Prodigal Daughter.

Back at the house, my mother asked me to write the eulogy. The thought of getting up to speak in a Catholic Church made me anxious and I pictured a crucifix bursting into flames and the stained glass windows shattering the moment I took the pulpit.

My father taught me how to ride a bike, I wrote in my notebook. *He taught me how to swim and drive a car.* He also put my head through my bedroom wall *twice.* I tried to imagine myself standing in front of my relatives in the church, spewing platitudes like, "he was the best father in the world." I would speak so unconvincingly that I would lose their attention. I couldn't rely on any of my typical cheap spoken-word tricks.

Cursing indiscriminately or showing my tits in a push-up bra were not going to cut it with this crowd. I would begin to stutter and it would all go downhill from there. A giant pimple busted out on my chin as I attempted to write about my father.

I stopped writing and checked my voicemail. Chris, the guy I'd been seeing left a few messages. He wasn't really my boyfriend and neither of us could admit it yet, but we were in love. This was complicated, since I was a lesbian. The night before, I dreamed that Chris had slept with The Junk Collector, who mid-dream morphed into my ex-girlfriend Jen, who had been sleeping with men behind my back throughout our relationship and had given me genital warts.

Chris and I had spoken after my father died and he passed the news on to some of our other friends. The condolences were piling up in my voicemail, but I didn't have the will to get back to anyone. He told me everyone missed me and he offered again to come to the wake. Others wanted to come as well, but over the years, I'd become adept at building a wall between my family and my friends. As much as I craved intimacy, I shunned it.

I told my mother I would not be giving a eulogy. She gave me The Look, but did not argue. Greg returned from the store with his new suit, which cost several hundred dollars, which he'd bought at Brooks Brothers with my mother's credit card. My mother didn't seem to notice the cost. He modeled it for us, along with his shiny new dress shoes.

"Very nice," my mother said, "You should dress like that more often."

My brother announced that he would be wearing the suit again. He would cut the sleeves off the jacket and wear it when he played with his improvisational jazz band.

Friends and neighbors began to arrive. My mother made coffee, but there was no food in the house. Weren't the visitors supposed to arrive with casseroles or some other edible offerings? I ordered some pizzas and salads over the phone and paid for everything when it arrived. It was easier to coordinate the group feeding than actually talk to those present. Still, I felt edgy and my hands were visibly shaking. I thought maybe I should have a drink, but since my father got sick, the fridge was stocked only with O'Doul's, the non-alcoholic beer. The liquor cabinet hadn't changed since I was in high school and contained only a solitary bottle of Crème de Menthe, which I was pretty sure was older than me.

My mother's aunt pointed at the pimple on my chin and noticed my shaking hand, "Look, she's so nervous, she got acne!"

I contemplated defending my complexion: "It's not acne, it's just ONE pimple," but instead I smiled. I would do a lot of smiling and not saying anything the next few days.

After the guests left, my brother said he was going to meet up with some friends. He asked me to come along, but I declined and he drove off in my father's car. I'd lost touch with my friends here years ago and knew there was no way my mother was going to let me drive her car so I headed up to my old room with a slice of mushroom pizza and an O'Doul's. I turned to my father's radio station—the oldies station—on my former boom box. When I was a kid, the sounds of doo-wop pumped through the house like a retro soundtrack. My father was big on the '50s music and spent weekends sitting at our kitchen table taping Cousin Brucie's Saturday Night Oldies Party, so he could listen to it throughout the week. This was a source of embarrassment to me during the summer, when with all the doors and windows open, the doo-wop would spew forth from our house, competing with what I called the "late '80's Guido rock" blasting from most of the cars on the highway. There was no need to buy tapes or albums, my father believed, if you could record everything off the radio.

I looked around my old room. It was bigger than most studio apartments I'd seen in Manhattan. I was never allowed to decorate it myself—my mother found rock posters "unfeminine." When I was a junior in high school, my mother decided to redecorate my room. Greg and I came home one day to find my room was now that putrid hotel shade of pink known as "dusty rose." Dusty rose curtains adorned the windows, and two of the walls were papered in a dusty rose floral print, the other two were covered in gray paneling.

Eating my pizza, I thought again about how my father had twice put my head through almost the exact same spot on one of the paneled walls behind the door. The first time was in the seventh grade while I was complaining about my lack of clothes. "That's what happens when you get as fat as a house," he said as he pushed me into the wall.

The wall was relatively hollow and my head went through it like a knife through cardboard. The hole was then fixed.

The second drama played out my junior year. I was kicked out of my Honors English class, which was taught by a woman I admired because of her stance as a self-described feminist. After telling me I had to report to regular English, she said to me, "the rest of the kids in this class need to concentrate on writing good essays for their college applications."

"Well, what about me?" I inquired. I had to write my college essays too.

"Oh, honey," she said condescendingly, "you're not going to go to college. At least not right away. There's always community college."

It was true, I was doing poorly in all my classes. Honors English was the only hope I had left and my teacher kept giving me D's. I'd never gotten D's in English before. Community college was for losers, losers like me.

My teacher smiled before hitting me with the number one backhanded fat girl compliment: "And make sure you tell your mother her daughter has a very pretty face." Then she turned in her feminist heels and walked away.

When my father lunged at me in the bathroom, after I cut myself, he grabbed me by my bleeding wrist and once again slammed me up against the wall behind the door, head first. I remember my mother helping me stand up and leading me to my bed. I looked up at my father as he stood in the doorway, his hand covered in my blood. He seemed upset, like he wanted to say something. But he just stood there and shook his head and sucked his teeth in a way that made me wonder whether he was ashamed of himself or of me.

I remember going to school the next day and being pulled out of my modified geometry class by Lynn, the guidance counselor—one of my least favorite people. All eyes were on me as I rose to follow her down the hall. I sat in her office and realized I was wearing the same sweater as the day before. This was a major high school fashion no-no.

"I heard you tried to do something to yourself last night," Lynn started.

"Yes, I did."

"And why did you do that?"

Because I'm 16 and I weigh 230 pounds. The doctor told me I have a thyroid problem and will never lose the weight. My father is abusive and my mother is overbearing.

You yourself told me I will never get into college and that I should look into a career as a tolltaker on the NJ Turnpike.

I am never going to have sex because when I walk by a group of boys I hear the words "disgusting", "fat fuck," and "look at the size of the stomach on that one."

I think I might like girls and I have a strong attraction to hallucinogenic drugs.

My mother sent me to a shrink who told me to look in the mirror and say to myself, "you're beautiful and people love you." Later the same day, while I was walking along the highway, someone in a car spat on me and called me a fat slob. Because it doesn't mater what I think of myself, I have no control over what happens to me.

I have a vision of myself in five years: I'm a 400-pound virgin living in my parent's basement, except they don't have a basement. When I think of the future, all I see is me not being able to fit into the tollbooth I'm supposed to work in. That's my future, Lynn.

That's my FUCKING FUTURE*!*

"I was feeling really bad."

"You know Cheryl, there are people in this world with worse problems than you," Lynn said.

That was the end of the discussion. I was sent home for the rest of the day and my mother, who worked as a secretary in another one of the town's schools, came to pick me up. She asked if Lynn had spoken with me.

"I hope you got that out of your system," my mother said.

Silly me. How dare I worry so much about my future! Who did I think I was? It probably does not surprise anyone to find out that following this experience, I increased experimenting with hallucinogenic drugs—trying to find an alternate universe, perhaps one in which I actually belonged.

As much of a fuck-up as I thought I was at 24, I prided myself on two things: my college degree and the fact that I would never live in my parents' non-existent basement. I cracked open my father's fake beer. He was right, it did not taste like the real thing. "In the Still of the Night" by the Five Satins comes over the radio. This was one of my father's favorites and was on frequent rotation on the oldies station. It's a love song, tinged with an edge of longing. My father once told me he wanted to be a songwriter, but the words got jumbled in his head. I laid on the floor of my old room, and let his beloved decade play through the night.

Each day of the wake, we commuted from New

Jersey to the funeral home in Staten Island. Greg drove us in my mother's car, one hand on the steering wheel, the other out the window, flicking ash off his cigarette. My mother sat in the passenger seat, also smoking out the window with one hand, while fluffing her hair with the other. I was in the backseat, the non-smoking petulant child, complaining about the dangers of second-hand smoke, "I'm blowing it out the window, for Chrissakes," my mother complained back. This didn't make much difference. My mother's cigarette smoke had a way of finding me, winding its way through heavily-populated Christmas dinners to locate me at the kids' table and hit me in the face. My feet were encased in the uncomfortable department store heels. At my mother's insistence, I wore nude knee-high pantyhose beneath my dress trousers. I always associated nude pantyhose with burglars. The knee-highs were suffocating my feet. I slipped the shoes off and wiggled my toes. My feet looked like they were about to commit armed robbery.

We arrived early to the wake the first day—before the rest of the visitors—to "spend some time with the body" as the funeral director put it. From the doorway of my father's room in the funeral home, I could see his profile peeking out of the coffin. My brother, mother and I entered the room together, but we were each on our own journey.

Just over a week before, I sat at my desk at work, contemplating margaritas during happy hour and jotting down ideas for poems in between entering data from publishing catalogs. I was particularly interested in reading the author's bios, figuring out how old each of them was, trying to gauge how long it would be until I was among their ranks. I spoke with my father from a pay phone at a bar later that evening, just a day before he slipped into the coma and he asked me if I had gotten into "that school," meaning Juilliard. "I haven't heard from them yet," I lied. This was the last conversation we had.

We stood in front of the coffin. My father seemed uncomfortable in his suit and tie and I wondered what he would think of all the makeup on his face. He was surrounded by flowers and pictures of him fishing. Although I watched him die, this was the first time I had seen him dead.

My mother and Greg were on either side of me, watching him expectantly as if we were waiting for him to do something typically unpredictable. I pictured him getting up, bursting out of his navy blue suit and busting shit up. He would scream at my mother before pushing me aside, calling me a name and grabbing my brother by the collar, just like the old days. As much as he terrified me, I wanted him to get up and fight. I wanted him to rebel against his $10,000 coffin. I wanted him to knock the floral arrangements off their metal stands. I wanted to be frightened by him, to hate him again. I wanted my father back.

His eyelids were covered in foundation. His skin was a sticky patina of tan, ruddy and pale. My father had very little facial hair. I remembered sitting on his lap as a little girl, running my fingers over his cheek and saying, "I love a man with a clean, close shave."

"They did a great job," my mother said, touching my father's face. I thought he looked horrible, like a plastic version of himself.

My brother was quiet, his hands inside the pockets

of his expensive new suit. The new Mr. Burke stood about a foot away from the coffin and leaned forward as if he were afraid to come into close contact with our father.

We sat in the front row of chairs as the visitors trickled in for the wake. The next few days went by quickly, a haze of family and friends. I stuck close to my godmother Bettina, who was not an actual relative. I was closer to her than to most of my kin. The rest of the crowd made me squeamish. I'd never been that close to my extended family and tried my best to alienate myself from most of the people with whom I shared a bloodline. And I was only out to my mother, brother, godmother and my uncle on my mother's side, and I dreaded telling people over and over again, "No, I do not have a boyfriend," although I sort of did. How was I supposed to explain to them that I was a lesbian who was now kind of dating a man? How did I explain that my last girlfriend smoked crack and gave me an STD and the girlfriend before that was twice my size and abusive? How did I explain that I was one of the only people in my family with a college degree and I worked in a bookstore? I had a lot of explaining to do and I was woefully unprepared.

Because of all this, I took a lot of walks around the block in my pain-inducing shoes. My family lived a short bike ride away from this funeral home until I was eleven and we moved to New Jersey. I would wheel around, lay my three-speed on the ground and pick up the flowers that had fallen off of discarded funeral arrangements, wondering if they had come into contact with a dead body. The flowers always looked too perfect—more like flower mannequins than actual plant life. One time, in elementary school, I came home from a bike ride with a candy bar tucked into the tight-fitting waistband of my shorts. My father noticed the candy bar and smacked me so hard my nose started to bleed. Snacks were closely monitored, since I was a fat girl. "You're not fat enough are you?" he screamed, "Huh?" My father spoke in questions—our communication always slanted toward interrogation. I wiped my nose but didn't say anything. I certainly was fat enough. I heard it every day from my teachers, my classmates, strangers on the street.

It was everybody's business how fat I was. I knew from experience the nosebleed would stop in a minute, my fatness would not. I later found the candy wrapper in the garbage.

At my father's wake, a strange man approaches me, "You must be Snapper's daughter, you're the spittin' image." Another one tells me: "Your face is a map of Ireland." I'm 24 years old and I've been told both of these things on many occasions.

I was sitting in the lounge of the funeral home, drinking from a bottle of water, wishing I could have a real drink, and I overheard two men talking about me.

"That's Snapper's daughter," one of them said, using my father's nickname.

"Looks just like him," the other guy observed. I glanced over at the men, who both looked as if they had just auditioned for bit parts in a Mafia movie. There were a lot of men like this at the wake, each a part of my father's past; fellow longshoreman, salt water fishermen, guys from the old neighborhood. I vaguely recognized some of them from long ago.

More than one approached me saying, "I haven't seen you since you were this high," holding a hand about two feet high. My father's friend, the one I nicknamed Dumbass Goumba and his wife, did not show up to the wake in person, but sent a floral arrangement, the largest one in the room. My mother was convinced they had called the local florist and asked the size of the biggest arrangement there and went one better.

In between viewings, we spent a lot of time at the diner. Diners were big with my family. Thanks to their large portions of practically anything, they were second only to the all-you-can-eat buffets my father treated like a house of worship. Food was what always brought us together. I tucked into my Greek salad, trying hard to steer conversations away from my love life and career. Some of my friends and a few of my co-workers at the bookstore had expressed interest in coming to the wake. The idea of this practically had me in hives. I was not used to mixing these two populations—my life in the city and my family. During most of my childhood and adolescence, I had few friends. After I came out in college, my mother was so afraid of the rest of my family discovering my "lifestyle" that I was not really able to bring my friends around.

The voicemails were piling up—I checked about every thirty minutes—everyone wondered how I was doing. I missed my cat, Sabrina who was being fed by The Junk Collector and defending her territory from kitten invasions. I missed the fluidity of my life in the city where I didn't have to worry about saying something off-color, where my clothing wasn't scrutinized, where I could drink after work, get up on stage and curse, where I could stay up all night writing. Or I could have sex with, and be confused by Chris, my new sort-of boyfriend.

I'd never understood dating. I spent my adolescence battling both anorexia and obesity and because of this I'd only been on a few dates in high school (when I was anorexic) and managed to lose my virginity to a 23-year-old amusement park attendee (when I was obese) right before my self-imposed deadline of "before graduation." In college, thanks to cheap beer, marijuana, hanging out at drag shows with my gay male best friend and an inexplicable, dramatic weight loss sophomore year, I became a full-fledged slut and once again skipped the whole dating thing.

On the day of the funeral, I put on the Macy's black and white houndstooth dress with matching black shrug sweater, black tights and the dreaded heels.

"Can't you wear normal pantyhose?" my mother said, glancing at my tights, but I'd broken out in hives the night before. The last thing I needed was to cover what was left of the hives in "flesh"-colored nylon.

There was a short service at the funeral parlor before we headed over to the church and then the cemetery, to "put him in the ground" as the funeral director had described it. At the end of the service, everyone in the room formed a line and went up to the coffin to pay their last respects. Since I was unable to come up with anything suitable to say at my father's church service, I was already feeling somewhat deficient, as if I'd really let him down. Earlier that morning I overhead one of his friends saying, "he sent her to school to be a writer and she can't even write a eulogy!" *That's right,* I thought, *I can't even do that.*

My mother, brother and I were at the end of the line, the last ones to say goodbye before they sealed the coffin. I had intellectualized the fact that this was only his body, that my father had been gone for a few days now. Despite this, I felt my face grow wet.

A procession of cars, headlights on, wound their way through the streets of Staten Island on the way to the church. I'd ridden in funeral cars before—when my grandparents and my father's aunts had died, but this time I had the feeling in the pit of my stomach that I used to get before poetry slams, a mix of adrenaline and absolute dread. I hadn't been inside of a Catholic church in two years—since my father's aunt died. As a child, I found churches both frightening and awe-inspiring, like a magical cavern full of bizarre relics. When we entered the church, my mother was asked who she would like to have carry "the gifts"—the wafers and wine that would be used for the communion. My mother said, "I want the kids to carry them." My brother automatically refused and my mother shot me The Look. She was not pleased that I would not be speaking at the service.

I said I would do it and my father's sister also volunteered. We headed to the front of the church. My father's coffin made its way up the center aisle, while being sprinkled with holy water and waved with incense by two altar boys. The priest wore green vestments, adorned with a Celtic cross. I noticed them when he reached the altar and began the sermon.

My parents were married in this church in 1970. My mother almost fainted on this very altar on her wedding day, in front of the waiting congregation. She had always explained this as pure nerves. Years later, she admitted to me she was having second thoughts about getting married. She was 28 and despite a surprising and successful career on Wall Street, she still lived with her parents. Her father had spent a small fortune on the wedding, her bridesmaids were dressed in chiffon and her wig was styled just right. Most of her friends were already married. So she rested in a chair, sucked it up and said "I do." In the wedding photos, my parents both look incredibly content—my mother all peaches and cream, my father all Marlon Brando in "On the Waterfront." My mother said she married him because she wanted to help him, to change him, and this inspired the only piece of relationship advice she ever gave me, "But you can't change anyone, always remember that."

My mother sat next to me in the pew. At 55, she was now a widow—a petite Italian lady dressed in black. I watched her watching the priest, eyes wide, as if she were viewing an unbelievable movie. I zoned out the sermon and looked at my father's coffin.

Through most of my childhood, my father often told of a nameless co-worker who had slaved to send his kids to college. The kids, in turn, stopped talking to him. "Can you believe it?" my father would say, "He put those kids through four years of college, and they do that to him." In the end, this co-worker died "with a body full of cancer." My father became fixated on this man whose children had forsaken him, whose body was overrun with disease. He told this story frequently, shaking his head, sucking his teeth.

This was his worst case scenario, the nightmare that followed him at every turn.

I managed to block out most of what the priest was saying, until I heard him utter the word "gay" and suddenly I found myself paying attention, afraid I was possibly being outed in front of everyone—*"he sent her to school to be a writer and she can't even write a eulogy...and she's a big bulldyke!"* But this was not the case, the priest was making an analogy between how unfair it was that my father had died so young and how unfair it was for another one of his parishioners that her son was gay. Hallelujah.

This statement directly had nothing to do with my father and me and yet it had everything to do with my father and me. It *was* unfair that he didn't know about this part of me. It was unfair of me of not to tell him and it was unfair of him to make it impossible for me to tell him. We were both headstrong and frightened others with our silence, we were both easily volatile and perpetually scared. This reserve, the inability to connect, I realized, this was my inheritance. Then I began to wonder if I was even gay any more? Did my sort-of relationship with a man make me any less of a homo? Was there a shelf-life on queerness?

My mother nudged me. It was time to bring up the gifts. My father's sister and I walked to the back of the church where she was handed the water and wine and I was handed the hosts in a ciborium. Much to my surprise and disappointment, it did not burst into flames the minute I touched it.

We turned around and made our way to the altar where the priest waited in front of my father's coffin, his arms outstretched. I became queasy and began to shake. I was afraid the lid would come off so I put one of my hands on top of it. I passed by my mother's cousin, who shook her head at my sight, and thinking maybe this was wrong way to hold the ciborium I took my hand off and the lid immediately began to rattle. I handed it off to Father Homophobe and went back to my seat.

After the service, we headed to the cemetery. When the procession of funeral cars left the church in the old neighborhood on the way to the burial, a group of men stood on a corner to honor my father. I wondered what their nicknames were. I made up some names for them as the limo we'd rented slowly rounded the corner. I christened one "Jimmy Two Shoes" because it looked like he was wearing two left shoes. I'd never met any of them, but they knew the secret of his nickname.

In the back of our limo, my brother looked at me and noted that the sermon was "kind of rough." My mother said she thought it was beautiful. I was silent. A short while later we were all throwing roses into my father's grave. This was when I was struck with an odd feeling that would soon become familiar; a rush of panic followed by an emptiness I needed to learn how to fill.

Later that summer, I got my own place, right up the street in Williamsburg, leaving behind the House of Hoarding. It was a 1-bedroom railroad flat that rented for $575 a month; more than I wanted to spend, but it was worth it to get away from the junk collector. I barely had enough stuff to fill one room. At night, I lay in bed, my cat Sabrina snuggled next to me and thought, "all this empty space is mine." I pushed forward and did my one-woman show, get back on the poetry circuit, refilled the Snapple bottle and got back to normal.

Chris and I settled into what we called a "girlfriend-boyfriend situation" that fall and he moved down the street from me. It's odd to show up at readings as a "lesbian poet" with a boyfriend in tow and I didn't feel comfortable with the level of entitlement I had as a seemingly heterosexual woman holding hands with Chris. This simple act erased part of my identity and we became another straight, white couple roaming the East Village drunk off their asses. AND I HATED that was what people saw. Whenever some dude on the street referred to me as Chris's wife, I wanted to scream, "I'm nobody's wife. I'm a friggin dyke!"

Then came the strange reaction to my new relationship from some of my straight female friends. For example, one friend brought a dinner party to a halt to announce my arrival, "This is Cheryl, she used to be a lesbian."

Or, at another gathering I attended with Chris, I was summoned to deliver some verse, " Cheryl's a lesbian poet, she writes lesbian things about lesbians."

Or, while walking down the street holding hands with Chris alongside The Junk Collector, she saw a filthy chair in the garbage that she wanted to take back to the apartment and said to me: "You carry the chair. You're a lesbian, you don't care what you look like."

Or, at a ladies night with a handful of straight friends, each of whom had experimented with women, some even with each other, this gem came sliding out: "Ew, bisexuality is so gross."

I looked at her.

"Well, I mean, you're straight now," she pleaded, unsure, "Right? Just like us."

"Don't you ever call me straight!" I snapped.

Or, once at an ecstasy soirée, a woman interrupted my making out with Chris to ask, "how did your mother feel when you told her you were gay?"

Or, at another gathering, a raging woman alternately scratched beneath her nose and shook her finger in my face, proclaiming: "You're just one of those lesbians who's going to use him up and throw him away!"

Or, the frequent and potent, "he's just a substitute for your father." While the other comments were ignorant and inflaming, they were almost laughable. This piece of amateur psychoanalysis, sometimes presented as a declarative statement, sometimes posed as a question, managed to slap me across the face. These comments came from a variety of women from many different areas of my life and as ignorant sounding as they were, they were right about one thing: I still identified as queer. Even the fact that I'd met Chris around the same time my father was diagnosed with cancer had not escaped my own amateur self-analysis. But, the constant public reminders by my largely liberal, otherwise non-homophobic straight female friends and acquaintances that I was a lesbian served to put my homo ass in its place.

One woman absolutely cheering for my relationship with Chris was my mother. To her, this was the most normal thing I'd ever done. When we visited her house at Christmas she let us sleep in the same bed (as visions of grandchildren danced in her head) so we didn't have to sneak around in the middle of the night.

Chris and I stayed together for two and half years.

8

Black & White

APPARENTLY, I WAS SUPPOSED TO MOVE IN WITH MY MOTHER. This seemed to be the consensus of the post-funeral reception goers. I was the oldest, the girl, this was my duty.

If I did not live at home, I should at least visit every weekend. My mother was going to be alone now. Someone needed to take care of her. It was as if this woman, who had just spent the last several months diligently caring for her dying husband while working a full-time job, had suddenly morphed into a 55-year-old baby. She did look fragile and had held onto my brother's arm throughout the burial. I'm sure she was exhausted, but there was no way I was going to move home. I agreed to stay with her for a week-and-a-half after the funeral, the most time I could get off from my job.

Early on in my 10-day sentence, Greg cut the sleeves off his Brooks Brothers suit and took my father's car to be outfitted with a brand-new sound system complete with speakers taking up half the trunk. He then packed the car with his clothes and expensive sneaker collection amid the dead man's rarely-used power tools and off-brand home stereo equipment. Greg then drove to Boulder, Colorado to use his inheritance money to open a hip-hop clothing store with some friends.

I sat around the dining room table that night, a mess of Thank You cards in front of me. I was in charge of placing a stamp on each envelope before it was stuffed. I enjoyed repetitive work like that, the kind that creates a rhythm, almost becoming meditative. I did this until I ran out of envelopes.

My mother walked in from the kitchen where she had been talking on the phone with one of her friends for almost an hour. She slapped an open card in front of me. "You're a writer, write something."

I was never one to follow proper etiquette. I had an aversion to cards, always feeling pressured to write something perfect. What does one write on a post-burial Thank You card? *"Thanks so much for coming to my dad's funeral. I had a blast! Can't wait to see you at the next one!"* The card was addressed to my parents' friends, an older couple who had spent an inordinate amount of time with them during my father's last months—more time than I did, I had been reminded more than once. I couldn't argue with this, I had definitely avoided the situation.

My mother saw me staring at the card, tapping my pen on the table. "Forget it. I'll do it myself," she said grabbing the card away from me. She quickly wrote something in her puffy, loopy handwriting. The phone rang again.

My mother had always been a champion talker, quick to fill every silence. I was more stoic, modeling myself after my father and not speaking more than needed to get my point across. As a teenager, despite my big Jersey hair and eye makeup, I was considered unfeminine, cold, like my father. This was the first thing she brought up when I came out to her when I was 21.

She came to visit one weekend and stayed with me in the East Village apartment I shared with a roommate. I invited a few friends over for dinner, and my mother made baked ziti for all of us. I'd been with my first girlfriend, Pam, for a few months. I'd never seriously dated anyone before, and was always looked upon with suspicion at family gatherings when I showed up alone. Pam and I went out of our way to avoid each other on baked ziti night, but my mother caught on. We were drying dishes after everyone else had left when she asked me if Pam and I were a couple. I said yes, indeed.

"How did you know?" I asked.

"I'm your mother, I know," she answered, adding, "I always thought you were a little masculine."

Even with my hair in a bob and dyed blue black, my skin powdered and remnants of pre-dinner red lipstick lining my lips, I did not meet my mother's standards of femininity.

"I don't mean you look a boy. I mean you act like one, like you have no emotions."

"I have emotions," I countered, my voice growing to the specific level of shrill only reached when fighting with my mother.

"No, I mean you're cold. Like a man."

This went on for longer than necessary. It was easier to debate my "masculinity" than deal with the fact that I was gay. It was how we operated. The argument continued in increments for years, but always with the same theme: how I turned out not to be what she expected. She didn't order the free-thinking lesbian daughter, she ordered the unquestioning, compliant daughter.

"You're going to think I'm crazy," my mother said, "but, I think I gave your father cancer."

I looked at her.

"No, really. Your father was out of control. All he did was scream at me and your brother, he had no patience. Sometimes it was like he was possessed, sometimes I thought he was going to kill your brother or me. I didn't know what to do. So I decided I needed to get a divorce and I remember I went out to the backyard in the rain and looked at the sky and asked God to please make it all stop and I felt him answer me, I really felt like he was telling me, *It will all be over soon*, and your father was diagnosed a few months later. I feel so guilty," she said.Even with an edge in her voice, she was calm and took a drag of her cigarette.

I didn't know what to say. The hospital my father died in wanted to do an autopsy to see how the cancer had spread through his body. My mother and I had an argument about this. She was against the autopsy, but I wanted them to dissect his head to see if they could figure out what type of mental illness he had. We were too much alike and I needed to know what was inherited and how much I'd picked up on my own. In the end, she won. No autopsy. No answer.

"You couldn't have wished it on him," I said, waving her smoke out of my face, "Keep smoking, we'll all have cancer soon."

"He had problems, your father," my mother said.

"Yes, I remember. I was there too. He went crazy on me as well, but you probably forgot about that. Not that you did anything to stop him."

There, I started it. This was the fight that we would always come back to for the next few years. My father physically and emotionally abused me for as long as I can remember, while my mother stood to the side. Then refused to acknowledge that what happened to me was abuse. She said that she and my brother were the real victims of my father's violence.

"There was something off in his head," my mother said. "He had a problem."

That became her standard answer: the phantom illness, unspecified and elusive. It was easier to blame something that might not even exist than admit that your family life was less than stellar.

Each day of The 10 Days brought back childhood's interminable sense of time—when every 24 hours was its own world, with its own battles to be won. I found myself falling into my old bad habits. I stood in front of the refrigerator with the door open for several moments at a time observing the well-stocked shelves, trying to figure out which bowl to stick my finger in, which item I would pick at.

Remnants of my father's illness remained in the refrigerator, some of his medication sat in a cardboard box, bottles of O'Doul's and cans of Ensure lined the shelves on the door. Apparently, that was all he could consume toward the end; fake beer and liquid meals.

My mother fell into her old patterns too. Whenever we were home together and I left her line of sight, she would call out my name repeatedly.

"Cher?" my mother would say, then immediately repeat it three times, "Cher, Cher, Cher..."

This would go on until I screamed, "*Whaaaat?!* Jesus Christ, you are *so* annoying!"

"I just wanted to know where you were. You don't have to be so fresh. Where are you?"

I would answer, curt and annoyed, "Why does where I am matter?"

"I'm just wondering. Jesus."

Pause.

"Cher? So, where are you?"

"Leave me alone."

"Geez, what's your problem?"

Fifteen minutes.

"Cher?"

"Whaaat!"

"Are you hungry?"

"No!"

"What do you want to eat?"

"NOTHING!"

Fifteen minutes.

"Cher?"

"What?"

"I want to eat something but I don't know what." The cycle continued.

My brother had destroyed the blue station wagon—the one that I had driven for a year and a half—a few weeks after he got his license. And my mother still wouldn't let me drive her car, so I had to be driven around like a child. During The 10 Days, she would pull up to the Cumberland Farms convenience store, and even though I was almost 25 and against cigarette smoking, she would tell me to stop being a brat and have me "run in" to buy her cigarettes, two packs of Kool Milds at a time. She no longer bought the whole carton, because she was always going to quit—*tomorrow*. She immediately lit up and the smoke found its way into my face, just like the old days. We made 10 trips to the Cumberland farms in as many days. One day, the clerk asked me for ID. I didn't have any on me, so I pointed to my mother waiting in her car at the curb, lighter in hand. "I'm 24 and they're for my mother," I said.

The clerk looked at me oddly, then relinquished the pack. When we lived in Staten Island when I was a kid, she would hand me a dollar and have me run to the corner store to buy her cigarettes. The store owners knew my family, and happily handed over a pack of smokes to a 6-year-old along with eleven cents change.

I'd strived to get my mother to stop smoking most of my life. When I was about ten, I decided I couldn't take my parents smoking anymore. At night their lungs performed a precarious ballet, their snoring and wheezing competing with each other for impact. So, I set off to sabotage their stash.

One Saturday night, while my parents and brother sat in the living room watching "The Love Boat," I pulled a stepstool in front of the tallest kitchen cabinet, climbed up and took down two cartons of my mother's Kools and three cartons of my father's Marlboros. I stood at the kitchen counter, opened each pack and shredded each cigarette.

First I broke the cigarette in half, rolled it between my fingers so the tobacco fell out and smashed the filter flat. I did this hundreds of times. This was a risky operation, as all either of my parents had to do was look toward the kitchen to catch me. But they and my little brother were too busy watching Captain Steubing flirt with Charo to pay me any mind. By the time the theme music for *Fantasy Island* began, I was hidden behind a volcano of shredded cigarettes. At this point, I realized I had no exit strategy. I knew I wanted the cigarettes gone, but I didn't know what I was going to do once I had destroyed them.

I pulled the garbage can out of the corner and began sliding the entire mess into the plastic lining being careful not to let any strands of tobacco hit the floor. I heard my father get up off his chair in the living room. Given his size, this was always a monumental action. I could hear him walk toward the kitchen. That's when I realized there was nowhere to run. I could make for the back door, but there were multiple locks. I would never get them all open in time. So I stood there frozen, behind a pile of tobacco, my chubby arms wrapped around my body awaiting my punishment.

My father did not hit me. But my parents both looked so disappointed you'd have thought I joined a gang that specialized in beating up old ladies.

"Oh, how could you?" my mother pleaded, "What were you thinking?"

"Jesus Christ, are you a fucking retard?" This was my father's favorite rhetorical question. He grabbed me by the back of my neck, "What's your problem?"

"Cigarettes don't grow on trees, you know," my mother said. "We're not rich."

I wanted to explain that I didn't want them to get sick, that I couldn't breathe at night, that my school uniform smelled like smoke, but before I could say anything, my father dragged me upstairs and threw me into my room. He slammed my door shut and yelled at me from the other side to not come out the rest of the night, "or else you're gonna get the belt."

My parents continued to smoke for years. My father quit cold turkey when I was in high school and started smoking again sporadically a few years later. After his heart attack, he quit altogether. For all of my substance abuse, cigarettes remained a second-hand habit. The sound of my parents' lungs crashing together in the night left an impression on me that I was never able to shake.

During The 10 Days After The Funeral, my mother and I packed up a good portion of my father's clothes to donate to the Salvation Army.

"What a shame," my mother repeated as we folded my father's big and tall work pants, his quilted flannel shirts and his white undershirts.

"This was how small he got," my mother said, holding up a long-sleeve t-shirt that looked to be comfortably my size, "It was like watching someone melt away."

I took the shirt out of her hands and held it up to my body. It was not much bigger than I was. My father wore shirts like this throughout most of his illness, and the last time I saw him at home, it seemed to swim around him like a blanket. I put the shirt aside, wore it to bed that night, and later took it back to Brooklyn with me.

During the 10 Days, we ate the food given to us by well-wishers. A group of my friends had sent us a package from Balducci's containing three casseroles. The printout accompanying the food read: Love and Support, then listed their names. The sight of the gourmet food made me cry. I missed my friends and had been shutting them out for weeks. I'd always kept to myself emotionally, finding most other people unreliable. Even then, with some friends practically begging me to share my grief, I couldn't let down my guard.

My mother cooked a casserole one night and as we ate, I repeatedly read through the names on the Balducci's printout. Besides Paula and Chris, they were mostly friends from theater and Judy, one of Paula's friends whom I did not like and who I was sure did not like me. I wondered why her name was on the gift.

I'd spent countless hours with said theater buddies, rehearsing my play "The Donut Hole," which was about a topless donut shop in New Jersey. The show ran on and off for a year at my friend Nancy's theater in Chelsea. My mother came to see the show one night and despite a plot-advancing cameo made by a strap-on dildo, she decided to bring my father and my godmother to see the play the following week. I was 23, and my father had never seen or read any of my work before. I had anxiety all that week.

Admission to the play included one free beer, which was purchased in bulk at a big box store in New Jersey. My nerves were such that I sucked down several beers before my parents and Bettina arrived. My anxiety rubbed off on Nancy and she started drinking as well. The family arrived. We sat them towards the front of the audience and gave my dad two cans of beer instead of one. Nancy and I sat in the back and watched them watching the show, bracing ourselves for my father's reaction to the dildo scene. I was not worried about the other two. My mother had already seen the play and Bettina loved a good dirty joke and was known for loudly announcing inappropriate things in public places. Nancy and I passed a bottle of Southern Comfort between us. I was afraid my father would do one or more of the following things: Storm out; Storm out cursing; say something rude to the actors; throw chairs.

The play began with two women wearing bras encrusted with giant donuts, kissing passionately. My mother and godmother were laughing from the first few lines. My father sat stoically, sipping his beer throughout. At one point one of the characters refers to "the catatonic troll wives gambling away in Atlantic City," and Bettina elbowed my mother, loudly cackling, "She's talking about you, Phyllis!" And my mother laughed even louder.

Soon, we were at the dildo scene, which was a humorous mind game between two young people of different classes. I took an extra long swig of Southern Comfort as my friend Paula, who played the teenage donut waitress, donned the strap-on and bent the actor, playing an overprivileged NYU film student, over the table. My mother and Bettina were laughing hard, covering their mouths and shaking their heads, even though I was sitting behind them I could picture the mascara running down their cheeks. My father sat solidly, but I noticed his shoulders were stiffly moving up and down; he was laughing! And even better, he didn't break anything!

After the play, the four of us went to a nearby restaurant. On the way, my father quietly told me he thought the play was funny, but I needed to write a musical, nobody wants to watch a play without singing. My mother and Bettina both said they were very impressed. "I can't believe you wrote all those words!" Bettina exclaimed.

While I was staying with my mother in New Jersey, my clothes were still in my closet in Williamsburg, so I was forced to take a trip to the local cheap clothing store, Mandee's, for some essentials. My mother dropped me off in front of the store like a seventh grader. I'd always had a mixed relationship with Mandee's which fluctuated with my weight and after an adolescence spent first battling anorexia, then obesity, I still longed to wear teeny-bopper clothing, items that wouldn't fit me when I was in high school, no matter how inappropriate they were rapidly becoming. Ever since I'd lost so much weight in college, I was obsessed with cheap clothing stores. A favorite personal challenge for me was to put together an entire outfit for under thirty dollars, including shoes and bag. This was hard to do in New York City, but I managed to pull it off more than once. I shopped at $10 stores, thrift stores and the Salvation Army.

Walking into Mandee's was like entering a portal to the past, where I spent more time checking out my fellow shoppers than what was hanging on the clothes racks. Even in 1997, big hair was still happening in central New Jersey. It wasn't as big as I'd remembered it from high school, but still reaching for the stars in the heavily-hair-sprayed style that Jersey girls were famous for. Perhaps this hairstyle was a hard habit to break or maybe after years of teasing, this was how their hair automatically styled itself.

I ran my fingers through my short dyed black bob, grateful that I'd lost my can of Aqua Net my freshman year of college. I paid for my new cheap clothes then waited outside for my mother to pick me up.

When I arrived back in New York after my duties at home, I felt both elated and disconcerted, the way I always did when I came back from New Jersey. But my extended stay this time added a level of giddiness to my return—I could have hugged the Port Authority. Back in Brooklyn, the apartment was as messy and disorganized as ever. My cat, or perhaps one of the many kittens, had peed on my modem and on my Candies' knock-off high-heeled sandals. I carefully sponged the modem, then washed the shoes, without getting the cat urine smell completely off of either. Not being able to afford replacements, I continued using the modem and yes, I continued to wear the pissy shoes. I sat down to relax on my futon and was quickly laid upon by Sabrina before the entire litter of kitten-beasts entered my room, lounging on every available surface.

Judy moved away a few weeks after my father died. She had a huge going-away party at a bar on Avenue B. I was still a bit shell-shocked from my father's death, but trying hard to get back into my normal life so I stopped by the party briefly to meet up with April and Chris. Chris and I still were not "officially" dating, but seeing each other. When I got to the party, Judy said that Chris had left and that April probably wouldn't show up until later in the evening. I thought this was odd, since I had planned to meet both of them there. Judy said it was great to see me, that she was *so* sorry to hear about my dad, that she wanted to buy me a drink. So I let her, thinking, *maybe she's not so bad after all*. She had signed the basket of food from Balducci's.

After a few cocktails at the going-away party, I began to loosen up. I chatted with a few of the people I knew as Judy kept plying me with drinks. It felt good to be out again, away from the funereal feel of my mother's house in New Jersey. It felt good to be drunk, back in my element. At one point Judy grabbed me by the hand and pulled me over to the bar's photo booth. She explained to me that she'd been taking pictures with all of her party guests. We mugged for the camera, sticking out our tongues and draping our arms around each other's shoulders. At one point, Judy kissed me full on the mouth with tongue and in one of the biggest drunken mistakes of my life, I grabbed her face and kissed her back. In the photo, it looked as if I were engaged in a supreme act of lust, as if I just couldn't help myself.

After the photo booth kissing incident, I decided to go back to my apartment in Williamsburg. It was 1 am and I was tired of waiting for April and upset that Chris left before I got there. I was also scheduled to do a one-woman show the following weekend that I had to finish writing. Judy asked if I was okay to go home, would I like to stay over on her couch, just a few blocks away? I assured her I was fine. She thanked me for coming to the party and ripped off one of the less incriminating booth photos and handed it to me, telling me she would keep the rest safely in her "New York" scrapbook.

After I performed my hastily written one-woman show to a crowd of six friends the following weekend, we headed to a local bar to celebrate. Chris and I sat separately from the rest of the group. He'd been avoiding me in the week between Judy's going-away party and the show. He reached under the table and held my hand. While the others talked around us, he confessed to sleeping with Judy.

"It was a mistake, a bad mistake," he said.

"Well, that's convenient, since she's left town. Did you like her?" I asked.

"No, really I don't. I didn't. I just wanted to touch her breasts, honestly. I was drunk. She was wearing this low-cut top and rubbing all over me."

"So, you're blaming the woman," I said, "You had nothing to do with it."

"No, it was totally my fault. I didn't mean it. Really, I just wanted to touch her boobs."

"And as you were touching her boobs, your penis just crawled out of your pants on its own and into her vagina."

"I'm sorry, really. Besides we weren't officially going out at the time."

"You know last week at her going-away party, the one you were conveniently absent from, I kissed her in the photo booth," I said, and immediately felt humiliated.

Then I realized why Judy had paid so much attention to me that night. She knew she had something on me—she had fucked the boy I was in love with.

9

Justify My Love

I AM ONLY ON MY THIRD STRIP CLUB AND ALREADY MY FEET ARE killing me. My job search has brought me all around midtown. It is early October, not quite warm nor cold and I alternate between sweating and shivering. I am currently heading downtown on highly-elevated foot to the third club on Shelly's list. Shelly is from Australia and she gives massages at a variety of strip joints throughout Manhattan. At the clubs, she wears a cute little corset-type costume and makes hundreds of dollars a night.

Shelly has already told me that I probably would not find work as a massage girl, but that I might get a job as a cocktail waitress. And at this point in my life, this sounds like a good prospect. Besides, it would be fun. I could wear a wig! It would be like performance art! So many women artists had worked in the sex industry and I was going to be one of them! Sort of.

Two and a half weeks earlier, on my 25th birthday, I quit my job at the NYU Book Center. The day before, my boss, whom I had come to secretly nickname ELB, short for "Evil Lesbian Bosss" had summoned me into her office to reprimand me. A professor had recently called to check on the book order for his class and as we were very busy, I had to put him on hold to help the customer with whom I was already on the phone. By the time I picked him up, he was screaming at me. "Nobody puts me on hold! Who the fuck do you think you are?" We'd had problems with this particular professor before so I was not surprised at his outburst, but it still shook me up. I held the phone away from my ear because he was screaming so loud. My co-worker looked over at me and shook her head.

"What's his problem?" she asked. He began complaining about the music we had "made" him listen to while he was on hold. He ended the tirade by calling me a "fucking cunt."

Somehow the boss was able to calm him down and I was promised by the bookstore powers-that-be that they would speak to the professor's department about his behavior. Ever since my father had died in July, I was an absolute mess. My mother was equally devastated and had been calling me at work frequently. My mother called me frequently in general; it was sort of an in-joke with friends and co-workers, but after my father died it reached a new high—her need factor was out of control. My co-workers were understanding. My boss, however, was another story.

The day before my 25th birthday, she called me into her office to show me a receipt for a special order that

I had incorrectly added up. The total was correct but she didn't like the way I itemized the books on the receipt. After reprimanding me for that, she again brought up the nasty professor episode, stating that the last thing they wanted was to lose professors to Barnes & Noble.

I reminded her that they were supposed to speak to the professor's department about him calling me a "fucking cunt." She fired back that if I hadn't put the professor on hold to talk to my mother, he wouldn't have called me a cunt to begin with. I told her my co-workers spent plenty of time on the phone with their husbands, babysitters, daycare. She said they were more important than I was. I went up to the bathroom, locked myself in a stall and cried for an hour. I had managed to squirrel away a few thousand dollars in the university credit union and my father had left me some money, so I would be financially okay for a while. I gave my two weeks notice the next day. On my last day of work, I was given a party in the break room.

My fellow bookstore clerks signed a card for me and there was a cake. ELB did not show up. She left a note on my desk the day before on a torn-off piece of green bar paper—the paper we used to print out sales reports. The note said, "good luck with your writing" and ELB signed her name. I was also presented with a copy of *Writer's Market* and was told ELB had suggested this as a going-away present. I graciously accepted the book and later, after several cocktails, tossed it in the trash. Even though my apartment was bursting with books I had purchased with my discount from the bookstore, I did not want anything that reminded me of my final weeks on the job. Some other aspiring writer would find it.

The granny boots on my feet were definitely not made for walking. They were black with a 4-inch stiletto heel and a spectator-style design across the front. I purchased them in a $10 store for $12 dollars one evening after a particularly bad day at work and several margaritas at Happy Hour. I promptly placed them in the back of my closet, and had pulled them out that morning to complete what I thought was a sexy outfit: short, black pleated skirt, fishnets, low-cut tank top and a rhinestone choker.

But as I caught my reflection in a store window, I realized my clothes and my full face of makeup were both incredibly bad choices. The eyeliner had pooled in the corner of my eyes, my mascara was running and the blush, which I'd had since I was 16, and hardly used over the years, made me look shocked. I did not look sexy, I looked like a parody of a sex worker. If you were to trade my thrift store leather jacket for a rabbit fur coat, I could have easily played a hooker on *Night Court*.

I was several yards away from my destination when my right heel got caught in a subway grate. As I jimmied my foot free, I noticed a group of young girls and their mothers waiting to go in to the matinee of the Broadway musical *Annie*. I had begged my parents to take me to see *Annie* during its first Broadway run in the 1970's. This did not happen, because they hated going into the city from Staten Island. Eventually I settled for seeing the movie version with my elderly aunts. I enjoyed it and liked spending time with my aunts, who got all dressed up to take me out. Afterwards we went to the fish 'n'chips place next to the movie theater and could see *Annie* played backwards on the wall adjoined to the screen. "Now you get to see it again," my aunt said, her fancy hat perched on her head as she happily munched on a piece of fried fish.

As I struggle against the subway grate, one of the little girls watches me precariously balancing on one leg, trying hard not to let my super short skirt ride up too high. I try to telepathically communicate with her: *Don't let this happen to you.* The girl's mother notices she's watching me and quickly shields her from the view. I don't blame the mother.

I finally get my right foot free by pulling it completely out of the boot, then pulling the boot out of the grate by hand. My sock is covered in a pattern of Scottish terriers, each wearing a fancy collar made of tiny metal studs. The terriers become animated as I limp over to a nearby wall and rest against it, and attempt to put the boot back on.

I have one of my little panic attacks, a surge of adrenaline followed by the emptiness. When my father died, it was as if someone had installed a switch inside of me that turned from numb to anger to desperation, stopping at various emotions in between, sometimes within the same hour. As I shove my foot back in the boot, I hover somewhere between anger and resentment. I gather myself and walk the few feet to the club's entrance. The doorman looked up at me.

"Hey, are you guys hiring waitresses?"

"You know a lot of young women come through here looking for jobs," the doorman says.

"Well, I'm one of them. May I go in to speak with the manager?" This was how Shelly had told me to approach each establishment. Since I was not with a man, I would probably not be let in unless I explained that I'm looking for a job. I was unsuccessful at the other two places and judging by the blank look on the doorman's face, this was going in the same direction.

"Wait here, I'll go get him."

Wow, at least the other two places let me in. I think about leaving, but I'm still hopeful. I'm trying my best to avoid going to a temp agency. The last thing I want right now is another mind-numbing office job.

When I started college at NYU seven years before, I opened a checking account at a bank near the campus. The man helping me with my application asked me what I was majoring in. "Dramatic writing," I answered. The man looked at and pointed to a picture of his two kids who looked to be 5 or 6, "I hope by the time these two are in college, they don't have majors like that anymore." At the time, I was appalled by his statement. But standing outside the strip club, I was beginning to think that perhaps the guy at the bank was on to something.

My father would not be proud. He started on the docks at age sixteen with an 8th grade education and stayed there for almost 40 years. He was proud of the fact that he never missed a day of work until he had a heart attack. When he was diagnosed with terminal cancer a year later, he wondered: "how am I supposed to go to work like this?"

And here I am, his only daughter, the first person in the family to go to college, practically begging for work in a tittie bar. I am the one with the fancy degree from NYU which has prepared me to do absolutely nothing of value in society. Years ago, when I told him I wanted to apply to college, he laughed it off as extravagant. "What do you think, you're better than me?" But standing outside the strip joint today in my clownish, slutty outfit, hoping for an easy day job so I can do my "art," wanting to join the ranks of female artists who came before me who worked in the sex industry to support their work, I have no doubt become an idiot in his eyes, what he would call an "educated fool."

The doorman returns. "No, Honey, I'm sorry, but you should come back..."

"When?" I hate when men call me Honey.

"Next week."

"Okay."

"You should definitely come back," he yells after me. As I am walking away from him I can feel his eyes on my ass.

I look at my watch: 3:30. I take Shelly's list out of the pocket of my leather jacket. There are four more clubs listed, the last being the one she worked in. I was supposed to work my way down to her club to meet her for a drink but I can't handle any more rejection today. My switch is almost fully turned to desperation so I board the subway and head directly to Shelly's club.

When I get there, I have to explain to the bouncer that I am a friend of Shelly's and that she is expecting me. Once inside, I can see that Shelly is massaging someone's shoulders. She smiles and nods in my direction, then mouths something I can't understand. I smile back and sit down at a table away from the stage where a glassy-eyed topless dancer makes her way down the catwalk. She's very pretty with a great body but she seems totally bored and disengaged from what she is doing. I look away and order a drink from the cocktail waitress, whom I study with more attention, since I would like to have her job. She's wearing a cute little costume and doesn't look to be much thinner or more buxom than me. I could fill her fishnets nicely. Shelly finishes up with her client and moves toward my table.

"Hi," she says in her sweet Australian accent, planting a kiss on my cheek, sitting down next to me, "How did it go today?"

"Nothing, absolutely nothing."

"Sometimes it takes a while. I asked here and they said they didn't need anyone right now."

"All I accomplished today was some major foot damage," I say, raising my foot to show her the granny boot. I notice the tip of the heel has been destroyed and part of the spectator design on the shoe is coming apart.

"I can't believe you actually walked around all day in those things," she says.

"Me neither."

The waitress brings my drink, I reach into my bag to pay her and Shelly stops me grabbing my hand, "it's on me."

"Thanks," I say. Shelly is sort of an "ex." We "sort of" dated last Spring. By "dated," I mean we went out drinking a lot and often wound up sleeping together. Ever since I started dating Chris, sex between us has stopped, but we're still good friends.

"So, how was your day?" I ask.

"Typical. Looked at naked girls, gave a few massages, had lunch, looked at more naked girls."

"It's a hard life," I say, downing half my drink.

"Oh no, it's Karen," Shelly says, hiding behind my shoulder blade. Shelly has a crush on Karen, one of the dancers.

"I think she can still see you," I say.

"I get so stupid around her," Shelly says.

"You must really like her," I offer.

Karen walks past us and flashes a smile. "Hey, ladies." It's easy to see why Shelly is both attracted to and intimidated by her. Karen must be in her early 30s, has long blond hair, beautiful skin and if I may indulge my inner straight guy, is built like a brick shithouse. Shelly lets out a long sigh and I join in with my own.

In one way, the club would be a nice place to work; good money and not particularly mind-numbing. There are music, drinks and, of course, the naked ladies.

Shelly certainly seems to like working here, but as I sit sipping my sweet cocktail and watching the girls spin around on poles, I get the feeling, for no reason in particular, that this is just not going to work out. I was still completely baffled, as I was with so many areas of my life, as to what I was supposed to be doing for a living.

When I get home later that evening, I pull out a forty of Budweiser, peel the granny boots off my feet and deposit them directly into the garbage bin. They are practically destroyed by now, half of each sole eaten away by pavement, the toes scuffed and several of the eyeholes torn out of their sockets.

I collapse onto my bed, my clothes still on. My cat, Sabrina, quickly joins me, purring next to me on the pillow. I reach under my bed and pick up my cordless phone to call my boyfriend Chris at work. He's currently working nights at a post-production house.

"Did you find something?" he asks.

"Negative," I say, sitting up and taking a large swig of beer, "I'm a tittie bar reject."

"That's too bad," Chris says, although he sounds relieved. I don't think he wanted me to work in a strip club.

"Well, Shelly told me about a few more I may go check out."

"Listen, I have to go but I'll call you later tonight."

"Okay."

"Love you."

"Love you, too."

I drink about half of the forty before laying back down. Between Sabrina's purring and all the beer, I am quickly lulled to sleep in my micro-mini and push-up bra.

When the phone rings 45 minutes later, I am startled and think it must be either Chris or my mother.

"Hello," I say, catching my breath.

"Hi, it's Judy," says the voice on the other end.

The voice sounds familiar and I scour my brain trying to place a Judy, when I realize I don't know anybody named Judy. I notice my left boob has popped out of the bra so I pop it back in and wait for Judy to explain herself. She doesn't.

"I'm sorry, who am I talking to?"

"It's Judy. April's friend."

I abruptly sit up. My feet hit the floor with a thump, and I become momentarily lightheaded. It's *that* Judy. The Judy who slept with my boyfriend the weekend before my father died. The Judy who slept with my boyfriend while my father lay comatose. The Judy who slept with my boyfriend while my father was in a coma. Did I mention Judy slept with my boyfriend?

I should just hang up, but I don't.

"Are you there?" Judy asks.

I take a deep breath and say, "yes, I'm here."

"Well, how are you?"

My feet are throbbing, a tiny, powerful headache is spreading across my forehead and my heart beats way too fast.

"I'm fine," I say. "Why are you calling?"

"You didn't ask me how I am," Judy says.

"Whatever."

"Well, you probably heard I'll be back in town next week," Judy explains. "Since I'll be in town and I just don't want there to be any drama between us. I mean I heard you were really upset about what happened between Chris and me. And I'm sorry it happened at such a bad time for you as well," Judy says. "And I know you had sort of a crush on me too, so that must have been really hard for you."

I feel like reaching into the phone and slapping her.

"What the fuck are you talking about?" I scream.

"The way you kissed me in the photo booth, I still have the picture you know. And the way you begged me to take you home at my going-away party. You're really cute, but I'm straight."

I want to get up and bang my head against the wall, but I can't move.

After Chris confessed to sleeping with Judy, he said, "I want it to be better between us. I want to be your boyfriend." After several more drinks and some tears, I agreed. Weeks of fighting over the incident ensued and we were finally in a good place in the relationship. And now this.

"Well, I guess since I've left town, he's been seeing you," Judy says with a quiet sigh, "That's why I wanted to call. I didn't want there to be any friction between us. We have similar friends. I didn't want it to be weird."

"Look, as far as I know, Chris wants nothing to do with you. And I certainly want nothing to do with you."

"I just spoke with him," she says, and I swear my heart skips a beat. Was he still talking to her? "And I think you have the wrong idea about our relationship."

I should just hang up now, but I feel numb, somehow suspended in time. It's as if I am observing this phone call from afar, like a bad accident on the highway involving a three car pileup and an oil spill.

"We'd been flirting for months," she says. But I already knew this.

"And, well that night, that Sunday night," I hadn't realized it happened on the Sunday night, the night before my father died. The night I spent with him in his hospital room while he was in a coma. For some reason, I pictured it happening on the Saturday night, not Sunday. This changes things.

"We were out drinking at my favorite bar, the one with the photo booth," she says, "and well, we started kissing there and he put his hand on my tits." I'm picturing Sunday night at the photo booth bar. The joint is sparsely populated, Chris and Judy are sitting together in the corner, they kiss, he feels her up.

"Then we go back to my place," I picture them walking down her long hallway, disrobing along the way, "and well, we were on my couch and he took off my panties."

I've been to her house for a party so I can picture it all a little too vividly. This is a bizarre form of phone sex. The sadism of her telling me what it was like to fuck my boyfriend while my father was in a coma, and the supreme masochism of my listening to her.

"Then he bent me over the couch," she continues talking, but I can't hear anything anymore. I stare dumbly at the wall. Sabrina tries to crawl into my lap and I push her away, grow lightheaded for a moment, then come to in time to hear Judy say, "and it was nice. It was really nice."

I put the phone on the floor. Judy is still talking, her voice piping through the phone. I press the flash button with my big toe and get back in bed. I am still wearing my pseudo-streetwalker getup and quickly strip down to my underwear and get under the covers.

The phone rings again. I let the machine answer. It's her again, saying she's sorry if she upset me, but she thought I should know the truth that it was only fair that I knew what really happened that night. I don't blame her completely for what happened and I know it's anti-feminist to hate another woman for what is essentially your mate's fault, but sometimes a fucking bitch is just a fucking bitch. She ends her message with "Peace."

I dial Chris at work.

"What's up?" he says.

"Guess who just called me?"

"Who?"

"Judy."

"Oh."

"Yeah, 'Oh'," I say, growing angry. "She gave me a blow-by-blow account of your rendezvous. No pun intended."

"I had a feeling she was going to do that."

"Why?"

"She called me too. She said she was coming to town and she didn't want any drama. I told her I didn't want to see her at all. I told her I was trying to work things out with you."

"Well, don't bother. Just go see her when she's here."

"Oh, come on. Don't be like that. I said I was sorry. I mean it. I really want nothing to do with her. I thought this was behind us. I thought we worked it out," he continues, "I told her I thought she was disgusting and that I was in love with you. That's why she told you all that stuff to get back at me. I'm sorry, I'm really sorry."

"Why didn't you tell me it happened on Sunday?"

"I don't know. You were having such a rough time. I didn't want to bring it up. I know how hard that was for you. Listen, can I come over later? I'll come over when I get off from work. I'll leave work early. I'll leave now. Okay?"

"Don't bother," I say and hang up the phone.

He calls back and leaves a message, then another. My mother calls, also leaves a message. I unplug the phone. I take a 2-liter bottle of Diet Coke out the refrigerator and put out food and water for the cat. I get back in bed, knocking over the forty of Bud, spilling the contents onto the floor. I don't clean it up. Sabrina sticks her paw in the mess before getting into bed.

At some point, Chris appears on the street in front of my building. He's shouting up to my fifth-floor apartment, "I'm sorry. I'm a jerk. I love you." I look out the window and watch him give my building super a note. Moments later, the super knocks on my door. I don't answer. He slips the note under my door. Chris' note has a picture of a guy labeled ME standing on the street with a dialogue bubble coming out of his mouth saying "I'm Sorry." I put the note under my bed with the phone. I take a sip of Diet Coke and get under the covers and I don't get out of bed for a day and a half. I don't leave my apartment for a week.

I don't go back to looking for work in a strip club, but I do sign up at a temp agency despite my aversion to office work. I also take a non-sexy waitress job in a café. I am lonely and after an intervention by April, many apologies and poorly drawn "I'm sorry" comics slipped beneath my door, I decide to get back together with Chris and we are very good to each other for a while.

I visit my mom one weekend in late October. We are eating cheese and crackers. At some point, my mother says, "these are the Balducci's crackers." I black out for a second at the table. I look at the crackers on the plate and all I can think of is Chris bending Judy over the couch. I run to the bathroom and throw up. I wonder if this is a sign of mental collapse: Patient associates sexual betrayal with and vomits upon sight of high-end crackers. My mother stands outside the door, "Honey are you okay? What, don't you like the Balducci's? It's from your friends. I thought it was so nice they sent something after your father died. They must really care about you."

All I can think of in this moment is a drag queen I saw perform years ago. She was nervous and a bit flustered and as her friends in the audience continued to good naturedly taunt her she said, "with friends like these, who needs a proctologist?" And with that the queen brought down the house.

10

Role Reversal

THE WEDDING IS MY BOYFRIEND'S IDEA. HE WANTS TO MEET MY family. Also, growing up Southern Baptist, he's never been to a wedding with alcohol and he is curious to see how that plays out. So when I tell him I've been invited to my second cousin's big day, he is eager to attend. He practically insists, "Come on, we have to go! I want to meet your people and this may be my only chance to go to a wedding in New Jersey," he says with an uncharacteristic enthusiasm.

"You know I hate weddings, especially in my family. Everyone does the Electric Slide!"

"That's why I want to go! My family doesn't do any of that," he continued.

"Okay, but when the time comes, you'll be the one sliding, not me," I said, "I hope you realize that."

My mother was overjoyed when I told her we'd be joining her at the wedding. I could imagine the wheels turning in her head: *Daughter actually wants to go to wedding! Bringing boyfriend! Must want to get married!* She'd just had surgery, which involved removing several polyps from her throat. The polyps had formed after 30 years of cigarette smoking. I had taken the day off from work and took the bus to New Jersey to drive her home from the hospital. I sat with her in her hospital room as we waited to find out if the growths were cancerous. She wasn't supposed to talk for a few days, but my mother is a non-stop verbal communicator. She never met a silence she couldn't conquer.

"I'm glad you're coming to the wedding." my mother whispered, her voice scratchy.

"Don't talk," I said, handing her my journal and a pen from my bag, "write it down."

She opened up the journal and started reading my next-to-last entry.

"Hey, no snooping, just write what you want to say!"

"You must really like this guy," she said, glancing at my previous journal entry.

I grabbed the journal away, ripped out an empty page and hand it to her.

"It was his idea to go. So you can thank Chris." I say, "I could care less."

But she pays no attention to me and is already scribbling a response, the non-verbal way of cutting me off.

"That means you must really like him," she wrote in her fluffy scrawl.

The doctor came in to look over my mother's chart.

"It's looking good, Mrs. Burke. We got all the polyps and it looks like everything is benign." I hug my mother. This is welcome news for both of us. The doctor looked at me on our way out, "Make sure your mother stops smoking or the next time she has something removed from her throat, it will be cancer."

I took the doctor's words seriously and while my mother was napping later that day, I went through all of her old secret spots, collecting the loose cigarettes she had nestled in the backs of cabinets and bottoms of drawers along with the Cadbury chocolate bars she worked hard to keep from us as kids. My brother and I have not lived at home for years now but my mother is still protecting her chocolate stash from our chubby, hungry reach, and hiding her cigarettes from my father, who quit smoking a year before he fell ill. When I found what I believed to be all of the hidden tobacco, I set to shredding the cigarettes into the garbage can.

My mother picks Chris and me up at the bus station to go to the wedding. Her car smells of fresh cigarette smoke.

"See, I've got the patch on," she says as she pulls up the blouse of her leopard print ensemble, exposing her fleshy arm, "And thanks to this little bitch," she points at me, "I have no more emergency cigarettes. Can you believe that Chris? She doesn't even trust her own mother."

"She's just worried about you," Chris says.

"Well, I can't trust you, that's the problem," I answer, indignant. Chris rolls his eyes, he's seen us fight one time too many.

"No fighting tonight. I've got the patch on. I'll be good," my mother offers.

After a telephone battle, we've already agreed to miss the church ceremony so we show up early to the reception. They've rented out a popular Jersey Shore restaurant where my family often ate when I was a kid. We liked the huge amount of food they served for such a low price and always went there when we were at the beach. We were also greedy, and there were times we drove an hour-and-a-half from our house in central New Jersey just so we could eat more food. I always ended the meal with a chocolate and pineapple sundae.

As we pull up to the restaurant, and I see its driftwood sign, I can taste the pineapple and the chocolate in my mouth.

Once inside, we find the proper banquet room. It's decorated in pastels; seafoam green and peach linens cover the tables, "Impressionist" seascapes adorn the walls. I am already having a bad time. We sit at our assigned table waiting for the others. My mother is scratching her elbows—something she does when she's craving a cigarette. Chris looks dashing but uncomfortable in his suit and keeps fiddling with his tie. I take out my compact and reapply my lipliner. The three of us sit there bored, uncomfortable, awkward and waiting to celebrate the nuptials of a cousin I hadn't seen or talked to in about 12 years.

My mother cannot take the silence and lack of cigarettes at once and bursts out: "So, Chris, do you want to get married someday?"

"Don't ask him that," I say, embarrassed. I don't want to get married and I have a feeling Chris does—someday, and not necessarily to me, but it's on his list of things to do.

"Why? Most normal people want to get married." my mother tells me.

Chris doesn't have a chance to answer.

"Oh, god, I wish I could have a cigarette!" she blurts.

I am 26 years old and Chris is my first boyfriend and the first date I've brought to a family function. This is not because I haven't dated before, but because prior to this I was a lesbian and therefore never had a boyfriend, nor was I welcome to bring any of my other partners to family events.

The bartender begins to set up shop and as I am already feeling tense and angry with myself for agreeing to come to the wedding, I immediately drift toward the bar. I ask for a margarita on the rocks, no salt—my drink. I also order a vodka tonic for Chris and a glass of wine and some ice for my mother. Halfway through the first drink, I start to think about how weddings are not unlike school: the arcane rules, assigned seats, barely edible food, the dress code. By the end of the second margarita, the other guests begin to arrive. It turns out we are seated at the "cousins" table, as the bride is my mother's cousin's daughter. So we are joined by my mother's other cousins and my uncle and his daughter Jamie, who is ten years younger than I am and who is wearing her prom gown. The sight of Jamie decked out in her prom finery reminds me that I am grossly underdressed in a glitter-encrusted velvet tank top, super short mini-skirt, fishnets and tall platform boots. It also reminds me that I never went to the Prom.

I order a third drink. One good thing about weddings: there's an open bar.

Chris is keeping an eye on me now. He knows it doesn't take much for me to fall into a drunken, depressed stupor. I retreat to the bathroom and take my drink with me. I lock myself in a stall, sit down and pee while continuing to sip on my drink. I am not happy. I stay in the bathroom awhile. By the time I return, the newlyweds have already made their entrance.

I sneak around the dance floor, where they are having their first dance and make my way back to my seat. Chris puts his hand on my shoulder. I look over at my mother who seems enraptured watching the happy couple while continuing to furiously scratch her elbows. I finish my drink as my second cousin, whom I hardly recognize, finishes up her first dance. This is swiftly followed by the father/daughter dance and even though I thought the liquor would brace me for the saccharine strains of "Daddy's Little Girl," I find myself with tears streaming down my face.

I'd never been the type of girl who dreamed of her wedding day. I had always laughed in the face of tradition, but the sight of my second cousin dancing with her father, fills me with a sadness so deep, there is literally an aching in my heart.

I had never been Daddy's Little Girl. Our relationship was cold and awkward. My father fluctuated between amiable aloofness and violence, turning in a moment from gentle giant to terrifying tyrant.

After he died, I slipped into an angry depression, what I later identified as a breakdown that lasted years. I drank to excess, turning mean and paranoid. I was incredibly needy but turned everyone away. I trusted no one, not even Chris, with whom I was in love. I was prone to crying fits. I once tried to punch out a store window in the East Village. The window won. I couldn't concentrate on my writing; instead I spent my creative energy putting together slutty outfits from $10 store offerings. I broke up with my best friend and was sure my other friends were all talking about how crazy I was behind my back. Basically, the world was conspiring against me. I was drowning in self-pity, cocaine and tequila. My self-diagnosed existential crisis was nothing more than a drug-fueled alcoholic rampage.

But tonight at my second cousin's wedding, it's different. Despite the alcohol, I feel as though I am truly in mourning, not so much for what I had lost, but for what never was. Chris begins to rub my shoulder, my mother looks over and sees that I am crying. She offers me a sympathetic frown while continuing to scratch her elbows.

The father/daughter dance lasts approximately one thousand years. The bar is on the other side of the dance floor and I've already drained my drink. So I sit there waiting for the dreadful song to end, my face growing wetter and redder by the second. The other cousins, most of whom I'd never met or hadn't seen since I was a small child, take notice of my state and begin whispering to each other.

When the song finally finishes, I head back to the bathroom, where I once again sit in a stall, this time fixing my makeup in my compact mirror. When I feel like I have covered the circles under my eyes with concealer and re-applied my lipstick and mascara, I make my way back to the party and go directly to the bar where I am met by Chris.

"Maybe you should take a break," he says.

"I told you I didn't want to come to this stupid wedding," I snort, "now we're stuck in goddamn New Jersey. I hate this fucking place." Angry Cheryl is surfacing and she is not pleased.

We both get another drink and sit back down.

"Eat your salad," my mother says, pointing at the plate t. The others are already working on their entrees. I make a face at my mother and push the lettuce leaves around. I take a bite of tomato, then carrot, then cucumber. Soon I have cleaned my salad plate and am presented with the "vegetarian option" which consists of a plate heaped with mashed potatoes, pasta in cream sauce and rice pilaf garnished with two green beans.

The band is in full swing and the "professional partiers"—hired to get the party started—are working the crowd, handing out inflated guitars. The guitars are quickly snapped up by my 80-year-old Aunt Molly and her silver-haired crew, who mime playing them while dancing with abandon. The sight of these tiny Italian-American widows getting down to the band's horrid rendition of "Blue Suede Shoes" is adorable and inspiring. I dive into the mashed potatoes and order a Diet Coke. I decide I don't want to turn into a total asshole tonight, I am going to sober up. Chris hands me a warm roll from the basket on the table, which he butters for me. *This isn't so bad,* I think, *I can do this.*

When the band begins playing "The Wanderer" and the emcee calls out the instructions for proper Electric Sliding, my mother and Jamie are already out on the dance floor, positioned at the end of the line, near the door. Jamie is one of the only cousins I'm close to, or at least one that I see on most family holidays.

Chris looks at me and says, "Come on, they're playing your song," before attempting to pull me out of my chair.

"Oh no," I say, still feeling drunk but getting it under control, "I told you I wasn't going to."

Chris shrugs and leaves me sitting there to join the line across the floor from my mom and Jean.

I watch in amusement as Chris struggles with the inane rules of the dance. I can't believe he is actually doing the Electric Slide. I wish I had a camera so I could embarrass him later on. I am so caught up watching Chris's dance moves that I almost miss my mom and Jamie leaving the banquet hall. Something is fishy and it smells like nicotine. I get up and follow them into the ladies room, where they have locked themselves in a stall. I crouch down and can see my cousin's 4-inch hot pink platform sandals, next to my mother's metallic gold wide-width dress shoes. Smoke is emitting from the top of the stall. Their giggling conversation completes the tableau.

"I feel like a criminal because we have to sneak around just to smoke," Jamie says.

"I know what you mean," my mother adds.

My 16-year-old cousin is hiding from her father. My 55-year-old mother is hiding from me. My mother is enabling a minor to smoke. My cousin is pushing my mother through death's door. And they are both laughing, as if nothing out of the ordinary is happening.

"Okay you two! I know what's going on in there," I feel like a geeky high school narc as I pound on the stall door but the phrase, "The next time she comes in here it will be cancer," reverberates through my mind.

"Oh, God it's her," my mother whines.

They flush the toilet and open the stall door.

"You," I point at my mother, "what the fuck are you doing? And you too for that matter, you're not supposed to be smoking," I say to my cousin. "You want to wind up like her?"

Jamie looks at my mother's puffy skin, pudgy middle and lined mouth. I'm not talking about the beauty implications of smoking, but she looks just like my mother did as a teenager so this gets to her.

"No," Jamie says, making her way out of the bathroom, possibly scared straight. "I can't believe you," I scream at my mother. "The doctor said you were going to die! Don't you care about anyone but yourself, you selfish bitch?"

This may sound like a harsh thing to say to one's mother, but we have been calling each other "bitch" since I was nine. It's practically a term of endearment.

"I'm sorry. Jesus Christ, I was just having a smoke. One smoke all night!"

"I thought you said you were wearing the patch."

"I am wearing the patch! It doesn't help."

"You're not supposed to smoke with the patch on."

"You don't know what it's like. You've never smoked."

"What do you mean? I inhaled your smoke until I left for college."

"You gotta loosen up. Go out and dance with your boyfriend. You're ignoring him."

My mother is great at changing the subject and she's almost sucked me in.

"What do you know about boyfriends? When was the last time you had a boyfriend?"

"I'm married!"

"He's dead!" I yell. "And soon you will be too if you don't stop with the fucking cigarettes."

I turn toward the mirror and my mother puts her hands on my shoulders.

Together, our reflection is startling. It's hard to tell which one of our outfits is tackier: my mother in her animal print mess or me in my cheap getup. One thing about us is clear; the apple has not fallen far from the tree. I start to laugh and cry at the same time. The bathroom door bursts open. The bride from the wedding in the restaurant's other banquet hall bustles in, followed by her mother. The bride is about my age and is also crying. Looks like the back of the bodice of her gown is torn and her mother stands behind her, holding it together ,trying to close the gaps with safety pins that are obviously way two small.

"Suck it in," the mother says. And the daughter holds her breath between sobs.

My mother watches with envy as the other mother tries and tries again to save her daughter's wedding.

"Oh, this is horrible," the bride cries out, pushing her mother's hand away.

I agree. This is horrible: two crying adult daughters, two mothers unable to console us. But in that moment, I realize for the first time that my mother and I were never going to give each other what we wanted. I am never going to get her to change her habits and she is never going to do the Electric Slide at my Jersey wedding. I share this observation with her and she replies, "Oh, but I hope you get married someday!"

By the time we return to the party, Chris is sitting at the table by himself. "These people are scaring me now," he says half-jokingly, pointing at the dance floor. The line dancing has ended and it's turned into a free-for-all of drunkenness. My mother joins my Aunt Molly on the dance floor, grabbing her inflatable guitar.

"I'm sorry I left you here. I caught my mother smoking in the ladies room with my cousin," I say.

"I figured something like that."

"She's never going to stop."

"You two look happier, or at least less hostile. That's good, because she does have to drive us home," Chris says.

My second cousin makes her way around the room to greet her guests, introduce her new husband and collect her envelopes. When she gets to me she says "Christine? God, I haven't seen you in so long!" then she hugs me.

I must look confused because she tries to correct herself.

"Oh, Sharon! I'm so sorry," she says, grabbing my forearm.

I don't say anything, just hand her the card with a check for a hundred bucks. She tucks the envelope under her arm before moving on to the next sucker.

While she walks away, Chris asks, "why didn't you say something?"

"It doesn't really matter who I am," I answer.

"Yes it does," he persists.

After all that's happened tonight, I decide I can be

Sharon. Sharon is the least of my problems. My eyes are puffy and my cheap clothing smells like smoke.

I'm full of starch and have that post-drunken bloat. My feet hurt and I've reapplied my mascara twice. But I guess that's pretty normal. Aren't you supposed to cry at weddings?

11

Drunksexual

AFTER A FEW YEARS TOGETHER, CHRIS AND I BROKE UP in the spring of 1999, this time for good. The reasons are too complicated to get into, but when we did, I turned to my recently acquired best friend booze. I'd always loved dive bars, so I started hanging out in my local Williamsburg joints, typically meeting up with a friend or two. One night, after a reading, I found myself lacking going-out-with-friends plans and I chose to visit a bar that was mostly straight, but very gay-friendly. While ordering my pint, I noticed several guys checking me out. I was wearing a t-shirt and jeans. I don't even think I had reapplied my lipstick. I hadn't come to cruise. I had hoped to run into a gaggle of friendly gay men to hang out with. I was in a hag kind of mood. But, there didn't seem to be any gays in attendance, just the hipster straight people. I sat down with my pint and shortly a guy came over and introduced himself. We conversed briefly as I slurped up the last of my beer. I knew I only had a few bucks left and was about to put on my jacket to leave when the guy asked me if I'd like another.

Why, yes I would, thanks. He seemed nice, or at least harmless and I didn't want to go home. I hated being alone those days, which is why I'd stopped off at the bar in the first place. He got up and I searched my purse hoping more cash would materialize. I only had three dollars, which I tried to hand to him when he returned.

"Hey, it's on me. That's why I offered."

"I really appreciate it," I said, taking a sip, finally realizing this guy was trying to pick me up. *So, this is the mating ritual of the heterosexual,* I thought. Of course, I'd hung out in plenty of straight bars before, but I was usually with a group of people or a girlfriend or Chris. This was a whole new situation for me; I was being read as a single, straight chick on the prowl and I chuckled. The guy and I finished our drinks, chatted some more and parted ways, saying we'd see each other around. We never did.

I was still depressed from the breakup and hated being alone. I tried drinking by myself at home, but that was too stereotypically alcoholic. So I continued to hit up the local dives, where I could drink by myself and still talk to people, and each time a guy would try to pick me up, sometimes more than one. I was overly aware of the sexual dynamics at work in the straight bar. I certainly didn't expect anyone else to pay for my drinks. I had a job and although I didn't make a huge amount of money, I could afford my own cocktails. Each time I accepted a drink from a guy I talked to, I offered to buy the next round, but they usually wouldn't let me. As a feminist, the whole setup was uncomfortable for me, but, as an alcoholic, it was hard to turn down free drinks. It was a battle between conviction and addiction; feminism versus alcoholism. The addiction always won.

The mood was completely different at the dyke bars, where I could sit for hours without anyone trying to talk to me. On the one hand, it added another layer of discontent to my whole "woman drinking alone in a bar" *mise en scene*, on the other I would have loved to get the level of attention from my fellow dykes that I did from straight guys at the Williamsburg bars. I refuse to make any pop culture analysis of this male/female divide, based solely on my own experience, but I will admit that during this period, I spent more time hanging out at the straight dive bars, where the attention I received, however substance-induced, was sadly welcome. With the debauchery, came the sex. Some with men, some with women, some with both. There were bar stool makeouts, dance floor antics, bathroom stall indiscretions and rooftop mischief. Sometimes it happened in my bed, but more often taking place halfway between the couch and the floor. I began to think of myself as a Drunksexual, just looking for someone with whom to be drunk and sexual.

A particularly classy gentleman once asked me, "do you like pussy or dick better?" And of course, I answered, "oh, please let me suck your dick right now!" Seriously though, even some of my more radical-minded acquaintances have a hard time understanding sexual identities that fall outside the gay/straight dichotomy. Percentages seem to help people get a good grasp on such concepts, so I will say I'm 85% lesbian, 15% bisexual, 100% Queer Dyke.

I begin drinking straight tequila and trolling the straight bars of Williamsburg to pick up dudes. I'd have preferred to be with women, but it's easier to meet men. Sometimes I'd go out with friends, but I could drink larger quantities if I was alone. Then, one night I ran into Keith on Avenue A while I was on my way to a writing group. I hadn't seen him in years. We reunited and I joined him back on the gay club scene, this time trading in our fruity homemade cocktails for drugs tucked into our shoes.

Finally, that fall of 1999, I joined up with two other women writers to form Jezebelle2000: The Glam Lit Tour and planned a five-week spoken word tour for the summer of 2000. I took on much of the publicity myself and begn to refer to being an independent artist as being a Part-time Rock Star. This helped keep my mind off the breakup, but didn't keep me away from partying. I drank and did lines at home before going out. I preferred the randomness of meeting strangers in bars to hanging out with established friends. *Sure,* I told myself, *I'm carrying tequila around in a Snapple Iced Tea bottle, but I'm planning a super-successful tour while holding down a full-time day job.*

My drinking soon progressed to the point of frequent blackouts.

12

My Extended Adolescence Officially Comes to an End

I'M FINISHING UP MY FIRST SEMESTER IN THE MFA PROGRAM at The New School when the call comes on a Friday in December in the late afternoon. Keith is in the hospital, with pain spreading throughout his abdomen.

"He may be admitted," Chelsea, his new girl pal tells me over my office phone. "He just wanted, I just wanted to let you know, I took him here. We're waiting for news."

Inside, I gasp *Oh my God*. Outwardly, I offer tell her in my professional phone voice, " I'll be there as soon as I can. Thanks for calling."

"There's no rush," Chelsea says, "I'm sure we'll be here for a while."

I start organizing the papers on my desk, unable to concentrate on what I was working on pre-phone call.

The waiting area seems more like a hospital-themed gay bar than an actual emergency room. Keith's extended group of friends are lounging in the vinyl chairs as comfortably as they would have on the giant white couches at Roxy, except that each one wears a look of concern on their faces. It's early evening and already dark outside. A stream of light fights its way in from the frosted windows and combines with the hospital's fluorescent lighting, creating a sort of mood light. And because it is a Friday night, some of those present are already dressed to go out, the vinyl pants and skin-tight, colorful baby doll tees lending themselves to a festive mood. Just another Friday night in the East Village. The smell, however, is undeniably antiseptic.

I have come to the hospital directly from work and as I stand in the doorway of the waiting area removing my outerwear, I am approached by several members of the entourage who hug and air kiss me in the European fashion—on both my cheeks. The last two to do this are Chelsea and Jon, who I quickly notice are holding hands They envelope me in a friendly three-point hug, familiar and uncomfortable. They sit down next to each other on the other side of the waiting room and hold hands.

I finish taking off my coat and plop down next to Brad." Look at you in these sexy pants," Brad says, practically lisping. He grabs my knee and begins to rub my satiny jeans. "Thanks," I say, "I aim to please."Brad continues the thigh massage as Jon and Chelsea intertwine their fingers across the way. It bothers me how bothered I am by this.

A white uniform fills the doorway asking for Jon, Chelsea and Cheryl. We three rise. Jon and Chelsea hold onto each other, walking directly behind the nurse. I follow them, holding onto my puffy coat. Thin, white curtains separate Keith from the next patient in the triage. One doctor is in there, maybe two. I don't know who tells us, the doctors or Keith himself, but I hear the words *Tumor. Possible. Cancer.*

A sharp pain spreads throughout my stomach and I become nauseous. Ovulation? Sympathy pains for Keith? The white coats leave and it is just the four of us behind the curtain, an antiseptic Oz.

"I need you guys to take care of me," Keith says.

Keith hadn't been close with his family for years.

We nod. Of course. We are there for him.

Jon slips one arm around Chelsea's waist, the other falls, like a buddy's, around my neck.

Behind the curtain, the tableau is Norman Rockwell with a dash of weird, the trinity is unholy. The caretakers have been naked together in a group and as pairs, they have touched the skin now covered by clothes, placed illicit potions where the sun don't shine, got on a hardwood floor to lick the icing off of cupcakes in the small hours of the morning, Jimi Hendrix coming out of a boom box in the corner. They have seen the sun rise on each other's nipples, stardust dance in the fine hairs of each beast's backside.

The caretakers have been a gang of three and a conspiracy of two:

Girl-Boy-Girl. Girl-Girl. Boy-Girl (both variations). The three caretakers group hug their sick friend, entangle the IV wires.

The others enter the treatment room. Brad is visibly upset and about to leave for the holidays. He writes down his contact information in Missouri. Hannah, who is actually married, or was at one point actually married to Keith for insurance purposes, fills out some official paperwork. More shiny queers appear, arriving as soon as they hear, filling the room with a bright energy.

I hear one nurse whisper to another, "I think they're all in a rock band."

Keith is assigned a room. Jon and Chelsea volunteer to stay at the hospital to get him settled. I leave with a few people to go to a diner. After a meal of tequila and french fries, mostly tequila, I head back to the hospital to discover I'm too late, visiting hours are over.

"My friend is in there and I'm one of his main caretakers," I declare to the guard, trying to sound official.

"Sorry, lady. Come back tomorrow morning," he motions toward the door.

"But," I begin.

"Tomorrow," he says still pointing at the exit.

Outside, I dial Jon's cell phone to see if he or Chelsea can come down to prove my necessity. It goes to voicemail several times.

I pace from the hospital to the curb and back again.

A man carrying a large box enters the hospital. I decide I will be able to sneak in behind the box. The guard is distracted, in a conversation with someone else in a uniform. I follow close behind the box man, almost make it to the elevators, then,

"Hey you! I already told you. Come back tomorrow."

"Sorry," I mumble on my way out.

Adrenalized, I hit the street, once again dialing Jon's number, Chelsea doesn't have a cell phone. I get the voicemail again. I don't want to be alone so I call more friends. More voicemail. I hang up each time without leaving a message. Frantic for connection or a hug or to break down in tears, I drift east. I'm not sure we're I'm going but I'll probably wind up at International or Meow Mix, where I might run into someone I know. This is how I connect to people—at bars, with a drink in hand. It seems impossible otherwise.

Why didn't Keith call me? I wonder as I walk down Avenue A. *Probably because I was at work and Chelsea was at home.* I'm sweating beneath all my layers and coat. I change course, heading west on 10th Street, and before I realize it I am on the grounds of St. Marks Church where my friend Regie hosts the Friday night reading at the Poetry Project. I typically avoid the Lord's house, but tonight something steers me to the altar of poetry.

Regie is busy getting things ready for the reading. He notices me at the door and waves me in.

"Hey, thanks for coming," he hugs me, completely enveloping me in his arms.

"I actually can't stay for the reading," I say, holding onto him. "I just needed a hug."

Regie pulls away and looks at me. He hands me the cup of wine he'd been drinking from and leads me into the kitchen.

"What's wrong?" he asks touching my arm.

"We think my friend Keith has cancer. Just found out a few hours ago."

"Oh, I'm sorry," he says, squeezing my hand, "that's horrible."

"He's still at the hospital. A few of my friends are there with him. I left to get dinner a few hours ago and can't get back in. I tried to sneak in behind a box and everything!"

"It's okay. Just calm down." He takes the empty wine cup from my hands and fills it again. "Here, have some more wine."

I take a Diet Coke-sized swig of wine.

Regie hugs me again, "Keith's such a good looking guy, too. Listen, I have to start the reading soon. Why don't you stay?"

I should just stay for the reading, go home afterwards, get up early and head back to the hospital for visiting hours. But I know that's not going to happen. I finish my wine, down another cup, thank Regie and leave. I walk back over to the hospital, stand across the street, looking up into the windows as if I could will myself into the building. I stand there for 15 minutes, in the cold, before getting on the L train.

Once back in Williamsburg, I stop at my local for a margarita, hold the ice and margarita mix. It's less harsh to think of the enormous amounts of straight, hard liquor I consume as "cocktails". The bar is quiet for a Friday night, but I look around for someone to chat/flirt/possibly make out with. No one seems to be there alone, besides me. I order two more "modified margaritas" and down them. When the spent lime wedge in my shot glass seems to smile back at me, I know it's time to go. I stumble home to not-sleep, a brand of drunken insomnia that can't play with the cat, denies logical thought, repels even the most entertaining late-night televangelists, the kind that can't even lift a glass to throw across the room. The type of funk that traps you in a room, with a blinding spotlight on the bed you made.

At dawn, I fill a backpack with essentials. I wash my face and brush my teeth, but I'm too impatient to shower. I apply deodorant on the subway, and not for the first time.

At First Avenue, I buy a bagel that I can't eat and coffee that goes down like water. I'm an hour too early for visiting hours so I sit in the bagel store and stare at my journal pages as if I could laser-eye the words onto paper. I order another coffee, as the old lady sitting across from me spoons a can of cat food onto a paper plate.

When I finally pass the hospital elevator force field and get to Keith's room.

"You look like a $2 whore on sale for $1.50," he says. And we begin.

13

All the Wrong Pills

"I'D LIKE A MARGARITA, WITH A DOUBLE SHOT," I SAID TO THE bartender, "but I don't want all those extra calories so hold the margarita mix and, um, the ice."

I really wanted two shots of tequila at once, but it seemed less typically alcoholic to order an actual drink. An after-work Happy Hour cocktail was normal; drinking hard liquor by oneself in an empty bar was not.

The bartender shook her head, "So you just want tequila straight up?"

I nodded.

"You got it," she said, filling two shot glasses and sliding them in my direction. She handed me a few slices of lime wrapped in a napkin.

Before I begin drinking, I turn around in my chair and flip through the jukebox's CD selection. I choose one of my favorite songs and return to the task at hand.

As I raise the first shot glass to my lips, Bob Dylan's "Idiot Wind" fills the air. During my junior year of college, I spent an entire depressed Spring Break week just a few blocks away, holed up in my dorm room, trying to stretch a dime bag ten days, figuring I could afford $1 worth of pot a day, and listening to "Blood on the Tracks" over and over again. Long revered by the lovelorn, cynics and depressives everywhere, it's the perfect album to just sit there and sigh in recognition to. The first shot of tequila cuts a path down my throat, spreading its familiar warmth throughout my body. I feel at home.

I missed my mother's New Jersey Christmas dinner because I am helping to take care of my Keith who is now undergoing chemotherapy for Non-Hodgkins Lymphoma.

Jon and Chelsea, with whom I had a three-way back in the fall, are sharing caretaking duties. As you can imagine, this makes for some awkward bedside manner. Keith was diagnosed with this particularly virulent form of cancer around the same time Madonna got married at Skibo Castle, few weeks before Christmas. I remember sitting on the corner of his bed as Chelsea read aloud details of the splendid affair as reported by *US Weekly*: the Stella McCartney dress, the haggis, Guy Ritchie's kilt. And I remember Keith saying with an overwhelming sadness, "Now whenever I think of Madonna getting married, I'm going to remember being diagnosed with cancer."

The caretaking, in addition to my full-time job and graduate school, has taken up all of my time, most of my brainpower and a good portion of my mental health.

I have prescribed myself a strict regiment of self-medication. Luckily, school is now on break so I have a little more time to play around with. Still, I take my daily dose. The second shot hits the back of my throat just as Bob Dylan sings my favorite lines: "I can't even touch the books you've read. Every time I crawl past your door I've been wishing I was somebody else instead." *How fucking brilliant is that?* I think and immediately turn around in my chair and set the song to play again.

I'm starting to loosen up and suddenly I'm looking forward to seeing my mother and brother the way a boxer can't wait to get in the ring. Mom was not pleased that I missed the holiday meal, but she was uncharacteristically understanding. She's had a soft spot for Keith ever since he sent her a postcard of himself in drag, shaking his ass on stage at the Pyramid Club. That was nine years ago.

I do my third shot as "Idiot Wind" begins to play for the second time. I look at my watch, it's 6:50 and I'm supposed to meet my kin at 7 at one of the Italian joints on Second Avenue by Fourth Street. There are four restaurants right on that corner so I thought I'd just meet them there and pick one. I quickly suit up and head back out into the cold January air. As I walk the few blocks to my destination, I notice there is a spring in my step, and an inner warmth that extends through my toes. I'm not drunk, just sort of even, and isn't this such a beautiful city? And aren't I lucky to live here? I walk quickly, determined to keep the cold at bay.

As I make my way up Fourth Street, I can see my mother and brother on the southwest corner. They are standing in front of my mother's dusty rose-colored Honda Accord. My mother is checking each of her car doors to make sure they are locked. My brother stands off to the side, one hand in the pocket of his oversize jeans, the other holding a cigarette. He's been living in Colorado and I haven't seen him in over a year. He's home visiting for the holidays. I quickly do the math; if I'm 28 then he must be 25.

They both seem so out of place standing there, like they don't fit into my life right now. Lately, my life has been running from my job to the hospital, from the hospital to whatever bar or after hours place I fancy. I don't sleep much these days. I barely slept much the night before and remembering this, I yawn. The cold air invades my mouth, working its way into the exposed root of one of my teeth, which I have ignored taking care of.

By the time I reach them, my mother is huddled under the awning of that corner's restaurant. She has just lit a cigarette and paces back and forth, smoking with one hand and holding a Christmas shopping bag in the other. She said she had some things for me. I've already told her that I didn't have time to buy presents for anyone.

They wave at me and suddenly I'm a bit frightened; is it obvious that I've been drinking? Do I smell like liquor? They don't seem to notice anything. My mother reaches over to kiss me. I can smell the cigarettes on her breath and I know that she'll leave an orange-brown mark on my cheek. My brother gives me a half hug and says, "Wassup?"

"Not much," I say and point them inside the nearest eatery as if that was the one I'd planned on.

As soon as we sit down, I order a vodka tonic. I don't even like vodka but for some reason this sounds like the proper drink for the moment. My mother orders a bottle of red wine for the table, for us to have with dinner, and my brother orders a beer. When our drinks come, my mother takes her fork and moves the ice from her water glass into her wine glass. My brother and I look at each other and roll our eyes.

"Ma, it's supposed to be room temperature," Greg says, laughing.

"But I like it cold," my mother says. At home, she keeps her box of red wine in the fridge and drinks it out of a small tumbler filled with ice. Unlike me, she's not a big drinker, she just enjoys a cold one every once in a while.

I look at my menu. I haven't been eating much the last few weeks and have been running mostly on coffee and the occasional order of french fries. That, and all the liquor—I don't skimp on the booze group. When the waiter comes to take our food order, I pick a fish entrée off the menu and ask for another vodka tonic. I drain my first drink and hand the glass to him. The salads arrive before my second drink does, so I pour myself a glass of wine.

"So, how's your apartment?" my mother asks.

"Okay," I say. My place is an absolute mess. There are piles of paper all over, dishes in the sink and my clothes are in disarray, covering my bedroom floor.

"And the cat?" My poor, neglected Sabrina. I always leave enough food and water for her but I've been lacking in the love department. Whenever I am home, she follows me around, meowing desperately.

"She's okay," I say.

"And the school. How's the school?"

"Good," I say. I'm in the MFA program at The New School, "I'm writing."

"What are you writing?" my brother asks.

"I'm writing a memoir about my horrible childhood," I joke.

My brother and I burst out laughing.

"Oh, you two!" my mother says, then to change the subject, "How's Keith?" My mother is very good at changing the subject.

"He's home now on a little break from the chemo. It's pretty intense," I say, and make a mental note to stop by his place after dinner even though I had promised myself a night off. He lives only a few blocks away.

"I remember how sick your father got, and he didn't even have chemo," she adds. "I wish you would've taken as much of an interest in your father's cancer as you do in your friend's."

It's time for me to change the subject. "This wine isn't very good," I say, finishing off my first glass just in time for my second vodka tonic. I've barely touched the salad but make sure to move the lettuce leaves around on the plate to make it look like there was some sort of action.

As we wait for the entrees, my mother pulls out the shopping bag. "Merry Christmas!" she says, handing it to me.

I'm a bit scared. My mother has really bad taste in gifts and I never know what to expect. Last year, she gave me several pieces of knockoff "Chanel" jewelry in gold and pearls. I have never worn gold or pearls. I've already promised myself to keep the sarcasm to a minimum.

The first present is an oddly-shaped and poorly-wrapped object which soon reveals itself as a ceramic leopard on the prowl.

"It's decorative," my mother offers, " You put it on your floor like a decoration. It will pull the room together."

"That's hideous," Greg says, almost choking on his beer—he's still on his first one.

"She has the leopard pillows," my mother protests. "It will match."

"Thanks," I say, not mentioning that the pillows she had given me, that were tiger-striped and I actually liked, were no longer in my possession. I threw up on one of them when I had the spins one night and the cat pissed on the other. I decide I will indeed put the leopard on the floor when I got home and wondered what Sabrina will think of this interloper.

The second gift is a pair of flannel pajamas, which, despite their hot pink color are completely wearable as soon as I remove the ruffles from around the wrists. The last gift is a small white jewelry box that looks familiar. Inside is a sapphire ring.

"It's my engagement ring, I had my diamond made into another ring," my mother says, holding up her hand for my inspection. "So, I wanted to give you the original. Your father would have wanted you to have it." That's why the box looks so familiar. My mother always kept it on her dresser.

I'm a bit dazed for a moment, a little swoony from the wine, tipsy from the tequila and the vodka. I realize giving me this ring is a sweet gesture, but I can't help reading into it: "I thought I'd give you my engagement ring, since you're never going to get married and have your own." I don't mention this, instead I remove a large silver ring from the middle finger of my left hand and slip on the engagement ring. It fits perfectly. Mom explains that she had the ring re-sized to fit my smaller fingers. The ring is white gold with a petite diamond-shaped sapphire. It's not really my style, but it's tasteful and unobtrusive.

"Thanks," I say and I mean it. I am on the verge of tears, but I don't let on instead I pour myself another glass of wine and continue to look at the ring.

I should have seen it coming. "Well, it was going to be yours when I died anyway," she says, doling out one of her other favorite sayings, "and I thought, why wait? She can enjoy it now."

After my father died, my mother became obsessed with her own death, constantly reminding me what I would acquire and what my responsibilities would be when her time came. She'd call me one day out of the blue and blurt, "If I die in a plane crash make sure you call my Visa card because I have travel insurance on that one." Or, once, when I was visiting for the weekend, she called me into the kitchen, had me sit down, looked at me solemnly and said, "I really need to know what you are going to do with the Christmas dishes when I'm dead." The dishes were white with a picture of a Christmas tree surrounded with gifts. She loved those Christmas dishes, cleaning them with a special cloth, keeping them packed in a box with our old baby clothes as cushioning between the layers of china. She unpacks them once a year for Christmas dinner and warns all those present against plate infractions.

I didn't want the dishes and told her so.

"They're Spode!" my mother cried out. "How can you not like them?"

"They're not really my style," I said.

"Fine. I'll leave them to your cousin then."

"She's not going to want them either," my inner brat yelled back.

I'm still looking at the sapphire ring as if I am waiting for it to come alive and tell me the meaning of life. I am beginning to get drunk.

The entrees arrive. My brother dives into his plate. The way he holds his fork reminds me of our father—how he used to shovel food into his mouth as if he were afraid the plate would run away. I realize my brother hasn't said much since we sat down. His silence also reminds me of our father.

"It took your father three years to pay off that ring," my mother says, cutting into her veal shank. My father was a longshoreman who worked 60-70 hours a week. Hundreds of hours of backbreaking, mind-numbing labor went into buying this ring. No wonder he was always so pissed off.

I look down at my food. A soft, pale mound of flounder sits innocently on my plate. I eat around it, spearing carrots and zucchini and taking small sips of my second vodka tonic. My mother and brother stop eating and look in my direction. This is it, I think. They've finally realized I'm a raving drunk. I feel a hand on my shoulder. At first I think it's the waiter but then the head attached to the hand bends down and kisses me on the cheek. It's Jon and I am momentarily confused.

"You said you'd be at one of the restaurants on this corner and I told you I would try to stop by on my way to Keith's," Jon says, before he, by way of introducing himself, kisses my mother's hand and slaps my brother on the back.

I remember our conversation earlier this afternoon, but I didn't think he'd actually show up.

"I looked in all the other windows, until I found you here," he says, smiling, "I must have looked crazy on the street."

"Jon, we already ordered," my mother says, smiling a little too much.

"That's okay Phyllis," Jon says, "I'm not hungry." They're already on a first-name basis.

"Want some wine?" I ask.

"Sure," I push my glass over to him and fill it to the brim.

"Get him a clean glass," my mother says. "You have germs."

"I do not have germs," I protest.

"We all have germs," she retorts.

"It's okay Mrs. B.," Jon says. I don't think I've ever heard anyone call my mother Mrs. B. before. Jon is really laying on the charm and my mother is soaking in it.

"Yes, we've exchanged multiple germs before," I add.

"Dude, that was totally unnecessary!" My brother finally says something.

My mother shakes her head and gives me The Look. The Look that lets me know she completely disapproves of whatever situation I happen to be in, The Look that makes me feel like I'm the scum of the earth.

"Whatever," I add.

After dinner, my brother and Jon begin talking about music and my mother pulls me aside as we head out to the street, "Is Jon gay?"

"No," I know what's coming next.

"Then why aren't you with him?"

"What? I've been with him. But we're not together," I know I'm being antagonistic, but I can't help myself after The Look.

"Where did you come from?" she asks.

"You shouldn't have smoked all those cigarettes while I was in the womb."

"Ma, come on. We gotta go." my brother is shaking the car keys.

"Your brother has a party to go to," Mom explains.

My brother comes over to our side of the car and hugs me and says, "catch you later." He shakes Jon's hand.

My mother kisses Jon on the cheek. Then looks at me, "Be good."

"Thanks for the ring," I say.

"Get home safe," she says before getting into the car.

Jon and I head east on Fourth Street to Keith's apartment. Jon takes hold of my Christmas shopping bag and I let him carry it for me. I really don't want to be seen with that thing anyway.

When we get to Keith's studio apartment, Chelsea is in the kitchenette, making him a peanut butter sandwich. After Jon and I de-coat she hugs each of us, and we each hug Keith, who is out of it, yet ironically clad in a t-shirt that says "On Drugs." We all settle around Keith's bed to watch him try to eat the sandwich. He takes a bite and chews far longer than necessary. Swallowing is obviously a chore that once accomplished, cannot be repeated. He pushes the plate aside.

"What have you been up to tonight?" Keith asks, his voice weak. Chelsea and Jon have gotten up and moved to the kitchenette, I can see them through the slats in Keith's decorative wood room dividers. Jon has his hands around Chelsea's waist.

I tell him about the dinner, the ceramic leopard, Jon showing up unexpectedly.

Then I show him the ring. "Does this mean you're engaged to your parents?" He jokes.

"I didn't think of it that way," I laugh, "but it is kind of weird." I actually think the whole gesture was sort of sweet on my mother's part but I don't say anything. My buzz is beginning to fade.

A line of pill bottles stretches across Keith's nightstand. I look over at them, so neatly organized by Chelsea. I haven't been too good at remembering the names of the drugs or their frequency of use, but this seems to be her area of expertise.

"I wish I could actually enjoy all the drugs that are in my body right now," Keith says looking over at his collection of meds.

"This will be over some day buddy and we can all party again," Jon says, suddenly reappearing at the foot of the bed. They've been friends since grade school. Chelsea comes in and sits to Keith's right. She is a new friend that Keith met at work. I look at us gathered around our sick friend. We are a twisted love triangle that began one night in this very apartment, when, after drinking pitcher after pitcher of a blue drink Keith had concocted, and snorting a large amount of cocaine, our usually playful and flirtatious interaction became sexually charged.

Before I knew it, Jon's hand was on the small of my back, my hand was on Chelsea's breast, Jon was kissing Chelsea and Keith was kicking us out of his apartment, "Okay, you guys have to relocate your heterosexual perv fest. It's time for me to leave for Roxy."

"Hey, I'm not hetero," I protested, "I'm bi."

"Whatever," Keith said flippantly, "you all have to leave. Now."

I was sitting between my cohorts and they were groping at each other from either side of me. What I meant to do was ask them in a low-key and offhanded way, "Hey do you guys want to come hang at my house?" But as I noticed the ferociousness of their fondling, I blurted out, "Let's go back to my house and all have sex!" "Sure!" Jon blurted back. Chelsea looked unsure, but nodded in agreement. On the way out the door, I saw Keith slip Jon a box of condoms and a Viagra. And the rest as they say, is history.

This transgression took place in November. And in the days since we have been together in various combinations: Chelsea and me, Jon and me. More recently, it's just been Chelsea and Jon, whom I think are officially "dating" based on an e-mail that Chelsea forwarded to our large group of mutual friends. The e-mail was from a friend of Chelsea's and contained various information about Keith's form of cancer, but at the very bottom was the original e-mail Chelsea had sent to her friend that referred to Jon as her boyfriend. The three of us have never come together again, except to take care of Keith, each taking turns staying with him in the hospital overnight, because he says we are all the family he needs.

"It just got so cold," Keith says, shivering. Chelsea, Jon and I look at each other. The temperature hasn't changed.

"Sorry kids, but I think the party's over. Who's staying with me tonight?" Keith asks.

"I am," Chelsea says.

"Oh good," Keith says. I get up to put on my coat.

"Goodnight, Cheryl," Keith says as I reach down to kiss him, "I love you."

"Love you too," I say.

Jon walks me to the door, "I think I'm going to stay here tonight."

"Oh, okay."

He tries to hug me but I keep my hands to the side.

"Oh, don't forget your Christmas presents!"

As he hands me the shopping bag and I have a vision of Jon and Chelsea fucking on the couch as Keith fitfully sleeps next to them.

Once out on the street, I am tempted to return to the International, but instead head for the L train back to Brooklyn. It's 11, I've totally lost my buzz and I decide I could use a good night's sleep. Halfway to the train, my cell phone rings. It's Joanie from England. Shit! I totally forgot I said she could stay with me tonight. Joanie is a friend of a friend who used to live in Brooklyn but moved back to England to detox from a heroin addiction. She's nice, but she talks incessantly and can be a handful. She's back in town for a visit and had been staying with my friend Dawn. Dawn has a date tonight, "Please Cheryl,

I really need my place to myself tonight," Dawn said. "Can you take Joanie, just for one night? Please?"

Dawn assured me that Joanie was off smack but that she still did blow, which she thought would be okay because I did blow too.

"Hello Love," Joanie talk-shouted in her Cockney accent, "I'm going to stay with you tonight!"

"Yes, that's great!" I lie.

"Where shall we meet?"

"Just meet me outside my building. You remember where I live? I'll be there in like twenty minutes."

"Well, can't I buy you a drink?"

Hmm, a drink. I should just go home, but I could use a drink if I'm going to deal with Joanie.

"Okay. Let's meet at the Greenpoint Tavern." At this point I'd have to completely start over to get buzzed again.

"Brilliant! See you soon love!"

By the time I get there, the bar is hopping. Joanie is nowhere in sight, so I stake out the one empty barstool and order a margarita; so much for the extra calories. I remember it's Thursday. I tell myself that I can stay out late; it's almost the weekend after all.

When I attempt to pay the bartender for my drink, she leans in and says, "the gentleman over there already paid for it." I look over. There are two guys sitting on the last two stools at the bar. One of the guys raises his glass to me. The seat next to him opens up so I make my way around the bar and sit down, dragging the Christmas bag along with me.

"Thanks for the drink," I say.

"No problem," he says. "My name is Jerry."

"I'm Cheryl," I say.

The friend pipes in, "I'm Stan."

"Hi." I wave over to him.

"You looked like you could use a drink." Jerry says.

"Yeah, I could always use a drink," I say. I want to add, "I think I'm an alcoholic," but I keep that information to myself.

"So what are you up to tonight?"

"I'm waiting for my friend," I say.

"Cool," Jerry says.

Jerry hands Stan a dollar. Stan gets up and heads over to the jukebox.

"We were just sitting here talking about how much you look like Gwen Stefani,"

Jerry says. "You must get that a lot."

I do get that a lot, especially since I dyed my hair platinum last summer.

"No, actually I've never heard that before. I'm flattered."

Stan returns from the jukebox.

"Did you do it?" Jerry asks him.

"Yep," Stan says, heading over to one of the booths to sit with another bleached blond.

I don't know what they're talking about and I don't ask. I finish up my margarita.

"Well, thanks for the drink. I'm going to go back over there and wait for my friend," I say.

"Hey, wait, listen," Jerry says, pointing at the ceiling. I look up and see nothing but the garish holiday decorations the bar is known for. Then I realize he is alluding to the sound system blaring "Just a Girl" by No Doubt. "I played it for you," Jerry says, "I played all her songs." I don't know whether to read this as sweet or creepy.

I'm starting to get my buzz back and suddenly Joanie is standing behind me.

"Hello, Love," Joanie says, reaching down to kiss me.

"Hi Joanie. How's your trip going?"

"Good, good. I'm glad I'm going to spend some time with you."

"Yes, me too," I lie. I wish I hadn't agreed to let Joanie stay with me. I wish I hadn't answered my phone earlier. *Note to self: Stop trying to help people.* My therapist says that I'm good at helping everyone but myself. That I mother others when what I really want is to be mothered. I usually don't listen to my therapist, sometimes I don't even know why I continue to see her, but I have to say, she's on to something here.

Joanie is super-friendly and is already introducing herself to Jerry and Stan, who order another round of drinks. Joanie pulls my old bar stool up and sits next to me.

"I'm going to order some party favors, do you want some?"

"How much?"

"I can get you a twenty dollar bag."

I take out my wallet. I have $44 to last me the next four days. "Sure, sounds good." I pull out a twenty and hand it to her.

"Brilliant!" Joanie grabs her cell phone and heads outside. I notice she isn't wearing her jacket and I call out after her, "Hey put something on! It's freezing outside." But before I know it, the door is swinging closed behind her. And I wonder briefly where she got the cell phone. Surely, her British cell phone can't work here. Then I wonder why I'm even wondering about this. Jerry hands me my second margarita and I quickly slurp down half of it. It's not quite midnight, still early. I tell myself I can get drunk again.

"Where did your friend go?" he asks.

"She went to meet her coke dealer to get us some supplies. Do you do coke?"

"No, not my thing."

Jerry asks me what I do for a living and I give him my standard answer—I work in an office in midtown but I'm also a writer, which is true and pretty much sums it up

"Cool," Jerry says, "I'm a bartender at The Q Bar."

"That's a gay bar," I say.

"Yes, but I'm not gay," he says defensively. "I mean I'm totally cool with it, obviously. But I'm not gay."

"I am," I say.

"Oh, um," Jerry stumbles.

"I'm bi," I offer.

"Oh, that's cool."

"Yes, I think so," I say with a renewed drunken confidence, "I think it's totally cool." I vacuum up the last drops of my margarita. Jerry notices my empty glass and quickly orders me another one.

"My ex-girlfriend said she was bi, but she never did anything about it," Jerry says.

"Is that why you broke up?"

"No," he laughs, "But I probably shouldn't tell you why we did."

"Oh, come on, you can tell me."

"Well, okay. She wouldn't let me spank her."

"Really, huh?"

"Yes."

"Is that something you're into?"

He laughs. "Yes, I mean it's not a necessity," he says, "but, yeah, yeah."

Most of my spanking experiences have been as the spanker, not the spankee, but I am intrigued nonetheless. I am also drunk, depressed and ever since Keith got sick, I've been sort of numb. I started taking Zoloft again on Christmas Eve after my therapist practically begged me to give it a shot. It does help with the depression, but I don't really have any emotions now. The prospect of feeling anything, even the cold, hard smack of a hand on my ass is welcome.

"You could spank me," I say in a whisper, immediately wishing I'd put it more coyly. I really have to work on my coy.

"Really?"

"Yeah, sure," I answer.

"Wow," he says, "Are you for real?"

"Yes, I sure am."

Joanie returns and hands me the tiniest Ziploc bag I've ever seen and I've seen a lot of tiny Ziploc bags. I feel a little cheated. I had expected more for my money. Jerry goes to the bathroom, patting my shoulder on the way.

"I know it's small, but it's the best stuff, believe me!" Joanie says, "Oh, I'm so glad we get to hang out together." She hugs me, pulling me a little too tight. I wish she would stop with the fake friendship display. I put the miniscule packet in the small, front, right pocket of my jeans.

"That's a good place for it," she says mysteriously, "What's going on? Do you fancy this guy?" motioning toward Jerry's empty bar stool.

"Not sure. But I might invite him to come back with us, if you don't mind."

"I don't mind at all. It's your place, Love," Joanie says.

Of course it's my place, I think and I can hear my therapist saying, "you have to stop getting permission from other people to live your life."

"He wants to give me a spanking," I blurt out, laughing.

"Oh my! What a night we have ahead of us!"

Jerry comes back from the bathroom, notices my glass is empty once again and orders another round.

I lean in and ask, "so, do you want to come back to my place? Joanie is staying with me and I thought we could all just go hang out there."

"Sure!" he says. "I'd love to."

When the final round of drinks arrive, I down mine without hesitation. I get a bit of a head rush and retreat to the bathroom. I look at myself in the mirror. I recently broke out in dermatitis around my mouth. I noticed the outbreak on New Year's Day, when I woke up in bed with Jon. The doctor says it's from stress. The cream he gave me seems to make it worse and looking at it now I notice it's spread to part of my cheeks. The makeup I applied this morning isn't doing much to cover it up. There is nothing I can do about it now, luckily the bar is dark, it's dark outside and I just won't put all my lights on when I get home. I take out the tiny plastic bag, and scoop an even tinier amount of coke onto the tip of my key. Joanie is right—it is pretty intense. As soon as I snort it, things become clearer, I am practically sober again.

I do not button my coat when we leave the bar. It's still freezing out but it doesn't bother me. Jerry is carrying my Christmas bag for me and Joanie is talking on her cell phone. When we return to my house, I set Joanie up on the couch, and say goodnight.

Jerr and I go into my bedroom, I close and lock door behind us. I never close this door, and Sabrina immediately begins scratching and meowing. It's hard, but I don't let her in. I know if I did, she would just want to be let out again. After a few moments, the scratching stops.

I'm nervous and want to do more coke. I need to loosen up but I feel awkward since he said he doesn't do it. I stand by my dresser, turning my new sapphire engagement ring over on my finger as Jerry sits on my bed on the opposite side of the room. He's flipping through a magazine that was on my floor. I am featured in the magazine along with the group I went on a reading tour with the previous summer.

I hope he doesn't notice the article, but it's too late. "Hey, that's you!' he exclaims, pointing at one of our publicity photos. I walk over and sit down next to him. I start telling him about the tour and describe each of my tour mates: what their work is like, how well we got along. He starts kissing me and we lay down on my bed. We make out for a minute when I hear more scratching at the door. I figure it's Sabrina again and ignore it. Joanie suddenly bursts in after jimmying the door open with a butter knife.

"Hey, what are you guys doing?" she asks, dumping the knife on my dresser. Jerry is on top of me. He quickly gets up.

I pull my shirt down, "Oh nothing," I say, "Is something wrong with the couch?"

"No, I just thought I'd come in here," Joanie says, her eyes glazed over. Before I know it, she is pulling off all of her clothes. They come off so quickly, as if they are held together by cheap Velcro. Within seconds she is completely naked. She walks over and drapes herself over Jerry's knee.

"I need a spanking," Joanie says, waving her ass in the air. I can't believe it, she's trying to steal my butt thunder.

Jerry is leaning back on the bed as if he is afraid to touch her. He looks at me, "what the fuck?"

"Maybe if you spank her, she'll leave us alone."

Jerry gives her a cursory tap, more of a grudge smack than a proper spank.

"Is that it?" Joanie asks, turning around to look at us.

"Yes, that's it," Jerry says.

"Well, okay, then," Joanie gets up, "I'm going to buy some cigarettes. Can I borrow your keys?"

"Sure, they're in my purse on the kitchen table."

"Thanks," she says, and slowly backs out of the room picking up her clothes along the way.

Jerry looks at me, "I know it's supposed to be really hot to have two girls at once but that was totally weird."

I agree. I look over at my clock radio. How did it get to be 4 am?

Jerry gets up and puts on his jacket, "Can I give you a rain check on the spanking?"

"Sure, I guess." I walk him to the door and watch him walk down the stairs. We do not exchange numbers.

Joanie returns with her cigarettes. I ask her to make sure she smokes directly out the window since I can't stand cigarette smoke in my apartment. She agrees. "Good night, Love," she says before settling in the windowsill in my living room.

I take off my pants and leave them on my bedroom floor. I climb into my bed and under the covers. Sabrina curls up next to me, purring wildly.

"This was a crazy night Sabrina," I say as I drift off to sleep.

I forget to set my alarm and jump out of bed in the morning. It's 9am. I'm supposed to be at work at 9:30. I call my office and tell them I'm going to be late.

My head is pounding and I stagger into the bathroom for some Advil. I notice that Joanie is gone. In her place is a pile of cigarettes on the windowsill, and a burned hole in the seat of my desk chair next to a Post-it that says "sorry" with an arrow pointing in the wrong direction. My keys are on the kitchen table, but the last $24 is missing from my wallet. Mysteriously, a brand-new box of herbal tea sits on my couch. I don't remember Joanie bringing that in but I guess she must have.

I go back into my bedroom and I search the tiny pocket of my jeans for my coke –thinking a little bump might straighten me out—and realize that is gone too. I have a flashback to Joanie saying last night, "that's a good place for it."

"Fuck!" I say out loud to no one. I really have to stop drinking. I mean it this time.

I notice the Christmas shopping bag sitting in the corner and I unpack the ceramic leopard, placing it in the middle of floor in the living room. Sabrina comes right over and sits directly in front of it as if challenging it to a duel. She raises her paw and smacks the leopard, watching it fall to its side before pouncing on the downed creature with a fierce velocity. It breaks to pieces which she continues to violently knock around on the floor. It's as if she is trying to kill something she knows all too well, something from deep inside of her. Before I leave for work, I pick up the pieces of ceramic leopard and along with the herbal tea, I put them in the garbage.

14

One Sunday Morning in January

I FELT AROUND FOR MY SHEETS, BUT COULDN'T LOCATE THEM. I pulled down last night's t-shirt as if it would do something to stop the cold, my thighs covered in goose bumps. Sabrina sat atop my chest. I felt her purring against my breastbone, her claws lightly kneading into me. She leaned closer to let out a forceful, stinky meow which I anthropomorphically translated to mean, "Bitch, my box is filthy and my bowls are empty. I can't even drink out of the goddamn toilet because that dude you brought home last night pissed in there and neglected to flush, so you best get your act together before I puke on your head." I didn't need to check on the particulars, this scenario has played itself out enough for me to know it was true.

The fire escape window was open, which explained the cold. I stood before it, Sabrina weaving between my calves, as Bedford Avenue collectively celebrated brunch. There was no gate separating the fire escape from my bedroom, I'd broken into my own apartment by crawling out my elderly neighbor's window and into mine on many locking-myself-out occasions. It was that kind of building. I closed the window, pulled down the blinds and silently thanked the dark goddess of alcoholic blackouts that Sabrina didn't decide to pack up her hobo sack and hit the road last night.

I ambled out to the kitchen, Sabrina dashing ahead of me. I washed and filled her bowls, left her there to chow. The seat was up in the bathroom, I had a flashback to sitting directly on the rim of the toilet. Was that a few hours ago or the other night? I put the seat down, tried to flush before I peed, but it wasn't cooperating, it did this every 10 flushes or so. I meant to call my landlord about this, but hadn't gotten around to it. I peed into the already yellow water. I'm amazed to find toilet paper. The litter box in the corner overflowed onto the floor. I got up, tried to flush again, already forgetting it was busted. I avoided the mirror, not ready for it yet, so I didn't wash my hands either.

I went into the living room where Sabrina was already on my computer chair, cleaning her paws post-meal. I sat in front of her, on the tip of the chair, as was our custom. I reached over to turn on my computer when I notice unfamiliar handwriting scribbled on the open poetry "ideas" notebook I kept on my desk.

Fun last night, it read. *I had to go this morning. Give me a call sometime. G. G?* I mentally gathered the various shards of the previous night and sifted through them for clues.

Ok, I was at a party for a friend of a friend in the city. I was invited to the party specifically to get my mind off the hospital and the easiest way to do that was to let myself fall down the hole again. Sitting on someone's bedroom floor chatting with a group of people. There were strong, clear vodka drinks, not my usual cocktail, but that's what was available. In a regular car, not a cab, maybe it was a cab, with three other people, crossing a bridge, Manhattan or Williamsburg? The skyline smeared, the water bounced, a series of shiny, slick knives below. An arm belonging to my friend's friend's friend, Gary, was around me—

Gary! That's *G!*

I couldn't remember entering my apartment, but I did recall sitting on the couch with him.

Back in the kitchen, I attempted to use the coffee maker, shakily filled the pot with water and wound up pouring most of it down the side of the machine. There were no coffee filters, so I arranged a takeout napkin in the basket. When I reached for the coffee in the otherwise bare cupboard, the can was empty. I scraped a spoon along the bottom anyway, as if that would conjure up some imaginary beans. I was alarmed at my lack of official hangover. I hadn't vomited, and didn't have a headache. Just a little shaky—and oh, yeah, I couldn't remember entire stretches of last night.

I pushed aside the coffee can to reach for the bottle of off-brand ibuprofen in my kitchen cabinet. I swallowed three tablets just in case and washed them down with the contents of an open, flat can of Diet Coke from my refrigerator door.

In the bathroom again, I checked my face. The rash

that had sprouted on New Year's Day had worsened, leaving tracks of raw skin from my nose to my lips on each side of my mouth. It was dermatitis. I looked it up online, in need of professional help, but I hadn't had a chance to go to the doctor.

I dabbed on concealer but it only flaked around the red edges of the dermatitis. I gave up on this and instead applied a dark fuchsia to my lips, which just intensified the scarlet areas around my mouth, and brought out the purple in the fresh hickeys on my neck while clashing with the yellow tones of the older ones. In my bleached-platinum hair, with the dark roots a few inches long, and frayed ends going in too many directions at once, I try for a sexy pout, but instead appear defiantly strung-out, as if the authorities have just closed down my meth lab.

"Looking good," I said to the stark mugshot staring back at me. I was still wearing yesterday's mascara.

I pulled on last night's jeans, a fresh bra and a soft acrylic sweater, which judging by its placement in the corner pile, I wore to sleep at the hospital the middle of last week. I zipped up my platform boots.

After a speedy blur on the J train, I found myself in front of an upscale Lower East Side joint. My friends Gina and Sally and my non-friend Karen were already there sipping mimosas. My shakes started pre-coffee, as the basket of mini-muffins was passed around. My companions seemed to be in good shape this Sunday morning, although they've all had to glue the heel back on the shoe many times in the past. In that moment they were my role models, ambassadors from the world outside the hospital, non-messes.

This is what savvy urban chicks in their late twenties did on Sunday; eat at a trendy brunch place, in cute clothes with clean hair and complexions free of scaly rashes.

I sat on my hands to keep them from shaking while I listened to the others talk. I didn't order a margarita. Coffee is served, food arrived, I still felt non-verbal. I both devoured and was disgusted by my yuppie omelet. But the faster I consumed, the less I shook. I couldn't remember the last time I ate.

"I slept with this guy and he never called me back," Karen began.

Maybe that's because you're a goddam bitch, I thought.

I'd developed a short fuse in the past month, unable to tolerate the normal minutiae of life. I ate with anger and wondered about the moments from last night that fell into the hole.

Gina and Sally offered Karen advice.

I was walking in on Keith's spinal tap as my father cried out, "I'm going to die" in the middle of the night. The two of them have morphed into a mythological, half-queen friend/half-Dad minotaur in my mind. The other day I stood outside the bathroom in Keith's hospital room, waiting to help him back to his bed when a nurse entered.

"Oh good, he's going to the bathroom. I need a stool sample," she said, handing me a plastic jar, before heading out.

Um, okay. Awkward. Stool sample. I turned the jar over in my hands, before knocking on the bathroom door.

"Dad," I inquired, before slapping my hand over my mouth. That was not the first time I had conflated the two of them, although it was the first time I had said it out loud.

"What?" Keith asked from inside the bathroom.

"Oh, um, the nurse needs a stool sample. I have the jar here. I'm just going to reach in and give it to you."

"I bet you never thought you'd have to ask me for a stool sample? Did you?" Keith joked as I handed off the container. It was one of his better treatment days.

Every day I spent in the hospital with Keith, I felt guilty about my non-participation in my father's caretaking. Whenever I helped Keith into bed, I pictured my father in his recliner, a once-tight sweatshirt pooling around him. I'm across the family room on the couch as if I don't want to get too close. When I shared veggie burgers from the outside world with Keith, I wondered why I never shared a non-alcoholic beer (the only kind he could drink in his last days) with my father.

Hunched over my place setting, I studied a few specks of rosemary, the only things left on my brunch plate. My hands had calmed down, but continued to shake slightly in my lap. Karen was still blabbing away about the dude. I missed the finer points of this brunch session due to my sickness and death revelry. I looked up to find Sally scrutinizing me from across the table, as if to ask, "are you okay?" I shot her a closed-mouth smile, but she still looked concerned.

Outside the restaurant, I quietly apologized to Gina, who had organized the brunch to get my mind off the hospital. "Sorry I wasn't all here today."

"Don't worry about it. I'm glad you came out. It was good to see you," she said, giving me a bear hug which practically lifted me off the ground. Karen and I half-waved to each other. Sally and I walked in the same direction. Always impeccable, she wore a cream-colored coat and tall brown boots, in which she was somehow able to maneuver around the massive puddles of melting snow. She also had bleached blond hair, but hers didn't look like she stuck her finger in an electrical outlet. We walked to a nearby store called Economy Candy where you could buy sweets in bulk.

I'd never been a huge candy eater, but I found the available variety intoxicating and I couldn't help myself. I was an alcoholic in a candy store. Chocolate-covered raisins, pretzels and peanuts, Twizzlers, black licorice, Jolly Ranchers. I kept throwing sugary items into my basket as if I were subconsciously planning a self-induced diabetic coma.

"I'm stocking up for winter," I said to Sally when we met up by the front of the store. She looked amused and I noticed that she had only picked up a few energy bars. I left the store swinging my bag like a well-adjusted little girl.

Back in my apartment, I emptied the entire contents of the litter box into a plastic bodega bag and filled the box with fresh litter. Sabrina immediately went in and started digging. I swept up, then decided to scrub the tub and sink. To my surprise, I had a scrub brush and a half container of Ajax under my bathroom sink. I got between the tiles in the shower. *Scrub, scrub, scrub.* I wiped the grime from behind the faucet on the sink and cleaned the bathroom mirror.

Quite pleased with the results, I moved on to the bedroom. All the bedding was on the floor to one side of my futon. I reached down to gather everything.

A Snapple Iced Tea bottle half-full of bottom-shelf tequila came rolling out, pulling along a cat hair constellation topped by a condom wrapper.

Further investigation beneath the bed uncovered several tiny Ziploc bags, completely scraped of their contents, a strapless bra I hadn't seen in a few months, assorted pretzel parts, an unfortunate family of Sabrina's half-mutilated freaky realistic mice toys and a miniature fortress of discarded condoms, mostly near the "guest" side of the bed. Not only had I been blacking out, acquiring facial rashes, neglecting my cat and sleeping with men I barely knew and rarely remembered, there was also a bad conceptual art factory beneath my bed. I stuck a broom beneath the futon to dismantle the installation.

Everything from under the bed went into a garbage bag inside of another garbage bag. I retrieved the emergency joints from my jewelry box and the pocket vial with tiny side spoon from my underwear drawer. I found the mirror, the old student ID, the cut-up crazy straws in my desk drawer, and the dime bag of coke nestled in the lining of a busted push-up bra in my armoire. I sprinkled the contents of the joints and the dime bag into the dark yellow toilet water, and felt a sense of accomplishment as it swirled and disappeared with the first lucky flush. The rest of the paraphernalia went into the double garbage bag, which I took outside to the trashcan along with the soiled cat litter.

The 40-ounce in my fridge was the first liquor down the kitchen drain, in a stream of prolonged makeouts, stoned philosophy and an endless Jimmy Page solo. You were my first and I will never forget you. Farewell, Budweiser.

The half-gallon of vodka, the mystical liquid that doesn't freeze, in my freezer went next in a slow, medicinal slink. I never enjoyed vodka, but at some point everyone started drinking martinis. They seemed glittery and sophisticated. Mature. Plus, I liked the challenge of a martini glass. I found gin completely repugnant so vodka martinis it was. The lesser of two evils escaped down the drain.

The prettiest vice lived atop the fridge in a sleek bottle. Remove the cork and it unleashed romance and poetry, lingerie and street fights, dinner conversations turned to tears. A warm, fuzzy downer generating brilliant ideas soon forgotten. A shallow magenta cloud filled the sink then disappeared.

Cuervo, I will miss you most of all, you crazy hallucinogenic bastard you. Yes, it wasn't your idea to pee on that roof that time, or show my boobs to the bartender on my 26th birthday for free drinks even after he'd been giving us free drinks all night, but you sure laid on the peer pressure and for that you must go.

I ripped open a bag of Swedish Fish as my final poison streamed down the drain. The kitchen smelled like my hangovers used to, back when I was an average drunk who got the spins and vomited in the morning. Back when I remembered everything from the night before, even things I wished I could forget.

When I was in high school, they took us on an excursion to a local drug-treatment facility to scare us straight. The patient in charge of showing us around was a middle-aged man who drank multiple cups of institutional coffee as he spoke. He was pale and doughy, an alcoholic. He told us his backstory, which I can't recall, but I do remember him telling us the facility allowed them to smoke cigarettes and encouraged them to drink coffee and eat chocolate, sort of transferring their addictive behaviors to other substances.

Over a decade later, I sat in my kitchen, nostalgic for puke and regret.

One month, I said, making a pact with myself, *your liver is on lockdown for thirty days and we'll take it from there.* I'd tried this tactic on myself before, to no avail, but I was willing to give it another go.

Finally, I said, opening a package of M&M's, my teeth sticky with Swedish Fish, *finally I've found a practical use for something I learned in high school.*

Afterword

I MET CHERYL IN 2004 ON A TUESDAY NIGHT AT THE ATOMIC Reading Series she was hosting in a Brooklyn Bar. I thought she was beautiful, very classy, and totally out of my league, but I flirted in what I hoped was an adorable fashion. She was polite and kind, as she was to everyone who read at her series, but she gave absolutely no indication of romantic or sexual interest.

We would periodically perform at the same events or run into each other on the street. She dated other people and when I noticed her Facebook status read "single" for what seemed like a respectable amount of time, I emailed her the traditional ambiguous lesbian social offer: a vague coffee invite. We had coffee, went to a mutual friend's one-woman show and then somehow ended up awkwardly and passionately making out in the back room of gay men's bar in the East Village. We both drank Red Bull and lapsed into stilted silences whenever we stopped the nerdy makeout session to get some air. Late in the evening, Cheryl said "So, um I guess this is definitely a date then," and we both laughed so hard that horny men stopped their cruising long enough to crane their heads around and see what the middle-aged dykes were laughing at.

It was like that with us—always the awkward laughter, always some juxtaposition, not quite fitting in. I am a round-faced, open-faced, Midwestern eater of all things beefy, she was a smart, hard-edged beautiful New Yorker down to her soul. We didn't really fit in with each other but we quickly learned to be each other's home.

We played a game we called "New York When," trying to remember what we were doing on a specific day in the '90s, she as a performance poet/artist and me as a Roman Catholic nun. When we discovered that on Thanksgiving 1994, I was delivering dinners to homebound senior citizens in the West Village while she did coke off a woman's ass at a house party not even a few blocks away, we mostly lost interest. There was no way to top that.

We fussed over each other in a way that neither of us had permitted a partner to fuss. I remember one spring morning she had made me a lunch to take to an all-day work meeting. She handed it to me as I walked out.

"I guess I have some Italian mom in me after all," she said, kissing me, and then added, "go wash your face again, you still smell like my pussy."

I started "so that's what Italian moms say—"

She cut me off, "Oh shut up."

And then a full five minutes of laughter, swelling, then fading, then swelling again. I leaned up against the door jamb, she sat on the kitchen floor.

It pleases me—as much as anything in this situation can be actually pleasing—to say that we were not a couple who ever took our relationship for granted. We knew what we had, knew how rare it was. We screwed hard and frequently and cuddled the shit out of each other. We had arguments but we knew how to deal with them and we didn't try to pretend that either one of us was not, in some ways, deeply broken.

It didn't take cancer for us to see what we had. We already fucking knew.

On January 21, 2011, a decade after she found a practical use for something she learned in high school, Cheryl wrote a blog post titled "Don't Bother, You're Going To Get Cancer Anyway."

Happy 10-year sober anniversary to me! My inner sarcastic cynical bitch returned to title this post. Funny and ironical, no? One decade ago today, I poured the last of my liquors down the kitchen drain and began eating candy—lots of it—to offset the alcohol sugar loss. I made a pledge to myself to sober up, taking it one month at a time. I tacked on another thirty days again and again until I made it to a year. I gained a little weight and it didn't bother me. I broke up with some party friends and I learned to spend time with myself—something I had feared before. Then I tacked on another year, and another year, until not drinking became as familiar to me as drinking had been. I had originally planned to have a big sober show/party for my 10-year, but, um, other things came up. In the mean time, I raise my coffee mug to you dear readers.

What came up was that Cheryl was diagnosed in October 2010 with Hodgkin's Lymphoma. She described what happened on October 29, 2010 :

Back in my days as a habitual club dweller, I closed down a number of venues. Frequently, I found myself the last girl standing at the dive bar or dance party or rooftop gathering or performance space and the first to suggest a trek to the nearest after-hours joint. Enchanted by the mysteries of NYC after dark, heavily self-medicated and lonely, I didn't want to ever go home. I was the girl in crooked heels, boasting cleavage inappropriate for sunrise while smiling smugly to myself, as if I had accomplished some great act of subversion.

Almost a decade of sobriety later, I find myself a partial homebody, who would describe an ideal night as a trip to the gym, followed by reading a good memoir and snuggling with my girlfriend. Who knew I would soon close down a radiology clinic?

It was Friday, early afternoon and I was busy throwing another batch of freshly updated resumes into the black hole of the current American economic situation. A few feet away on my nightstand, my cell phone rang. I didn't pick it up, mostly out of laziness and typically, it's my mother on the other end. I let it go to voice mail, which I checked about ten minutes later hoping for a job interview offer or something equally promising. It was the physician's assistant at my allergist's office asking me to immediately return her call. She even left her cell phone number.

The allergist had just diagnosed me with a lung issue called reactive pulmonary disorder, which is treatable with an expensive medication I had spent several hours earlier that week arguing with my insurance company to cover. They wouldn't. I was also being treated for asthma, the diagnosis for which was negligible. To be diligent, she also sent me for a chest x-ray. I had had the x-ray Thursday evening at a clinic on Union Square and treated myself to Artichoke pizza afterward. Then went to Trader Joe's, for some grocery necessities and went home feeling good about taking care of myself inside and out.

As I dialed the physician's assistant, I glanced at my to-do list: Job Applications! Make pasta salad for potluck tonight—buy olives, grated cheese. Pick out accessories to wear to wedding tomorrow—shoes, earrings, necklace (seriously on my to-do list). Print handouts for class.

The physician's assistant sounded nervous, as if she were about to ask me on a date.

"Are you in the city?" she asked.
"No," I said.
"You're not away, are you?" she asked, panicky.
"No, I'm in my apartment in Brooklyn," I said.
"I hate to tell you this over the phone. We got your x-rays back from the lab and it looks like you have a mediastinal mass, which is near your lungs."

I wrote "mediastinal" on my to-do list next to "Job Applications!" This didn't sound good.

"You need to have a CT Scan. It's possible this could be lymphoma. I'm trying to set up an appointment for you later today."

I wrote "CT Scan" below "print handouts." I was robotic, taking notes to share with my girlfriend, who's an RN and can decipher these things. CT Scan was now officially on list of things to do.

"Ok," I said. "I can do that."
"The tumor is quite large, about 17 by 15 by 12 centimeters. I'm going to make an appointment for you to see Dr. Levy early next week as well."
"Ok. Um, what kind of doctor is he?" I asked, simultaneously looking him up on my health insurance's website to make sure he was covered.
"Oncologist," she said.

Oncologist, I thought. That means cancer.

A rush of anxiety took over my body, followed by adrenaline. It was the same feeling I had had at my father's burial and when my mother had a stroke a few years ago. She survived, but there were several hours I was sure she had died. My whole body turned numb and I became focused on the smallest details, re-reading the to-do list, olives, grated cheese, telling myself I could bring the pasta salad with me to the CT Scan. I'll just put it in a sturdy container.

"Are you okay?" she asked. "I know this is hard to take in."
I realized I'd been silent. "Yes," I'm fine.
"I really didn't want to tell you this over the phone. I'm sorry we couldn't meet in person."
"Oh, no. It's no problem. I understand," I said.

There were more such phone calls back and forth between us that afternoon as she scheduled me for appointments.

She continued to say she was sorry and asked me if I was okay.

At some point, I gave up on the pasta salad and the job applications! I picked out my accessories. Called my girlfriend, Kelli, who at first calmy said, "Oh, okay. I'm coming with you tonight, honey."

I wanted to call my mom, but did not want to deal with her reaction, so I called my brother. His response, when I told him that I might have cancer, "Holy Shit. What the f***. Holy shit. What the f***. Holy Shit. What the f***." And repeat. I made him promise not to tell our mother until I was ready.

Kelli arrived, followed a few minutes later by her friend who had also had Hodgkin's years ago. Kelli had mentioned the scan to her friend and told her the approximate area of the clinic, which she Googled and showed up at the last minute to support me. I would have cried in appreciation had I not still been so numb.

After a long wait, I finally entered the CT room, where I was told to lie on a bed attached to what looked like the dissection of a space ship. As I settled onto the sheets and pillow in my hospital gown, I couldn't help but worry about picking up bed bugs. Seriously, when I say I was emotionally numb, I mean emotionally numb. A technician then came at me with an I.V. The bed was raised and automatically moved through the circular machine. I didn't realize the doctor and tech had left the room. A disembodied female robot voice instructed me to "Breathe in, hold it." Creepy. I did as the machine said. The bed went back to its original position and the humans were again at my side. The doctor told me he was going to administer the contrast dye and that I would feel a warm, tingly sensation, particularly in the groin. Even creepier.

Back in the day, the E would hit you like soft bricks and tiny explosions of heat traveled through your body and everything became brighter, more detailed as if you could actually feel objects through your eyes. Skin made tactile, a light sweat would break, the internal house music blasting, everyone was beautiful.

Sensations ended, the robot voice again told me to "breathe in." Soon it was all over and I was back in the waiting room with Kelli and our friend. We sat there chatting for a few moments, as the maintenance crew began to clean around us. Hint not taken, the receptionist, who was shutting down her computer said, "You're all set. Have a good night."

"I believe we may have closed the radiology lab," I said as we put on our coats to go outside. "This is a first even for me."

Cheryl describes the weekend after the first CT scan:

[Over the weekend] I grew even antsier, if that's even a word. A trip to Sephora could not calm me down. When I was told they were out of the lipstick shade I shouldn't have been trying to purchase anyway, I felt as if I'd faced a major rejection. Kelli and I got on a bus going downtown. I was silent, almost in a trance as we bumped along. She asked me how I was feeling.
"I want to run away. Just get in a car and go somewhere."

As I said these words I realized that unlike the other problems in my life I'd fantasized running away from: seeming artistic failure, crappy relationships, family crazy, flaky friends, NYC bar culture, NYC itself, the resume black hole and various other bullshit, this was one thing I could not distance myself from. I never actually tried to run away from the others, but the option was there. This time, my foil was inside me, literally. I could not run from it.

I settled on a mani/pedi instead.

Cheryl was scared and in some ways shut down, but I remember that Sunday her high-fiving a writer friend who asked how she was doing, "All I know is that I'm getting a damn book deal out of this."

Later I ran out to get some groceries and Cheryl texted me while I juggled the cranberry juice and organic applesauce: "Do you think my blog should be *wtfcancer* or *wtfcancerdiaries*?" By the time I returned to the apartment, she had already bought the domain name and was tinkering with the theme for WordPress.

"Well that's a new world record for Shortest Time Between Diagnosis of Serious Disease and Creation of Disease-Related Blog," I said, probably too cheerfully. She rolled her eyes, her preferred method of nonverbal communication. "Um, yeah."

The next week as she went through the post-diagnosis, pre-treatment boot camp of medical tests, she wrote constantly. She described her bone marrow biopsy:

My bone marrow biopsy was at the very least, the most ominous-sounding procedure on the menu the week before I started chemo. It turned out the pleasant young female doctor oncologist I met the previous, when she professed an affinity for such deep extractions, would do the honors right in the office.

Kelli and I arrived early for the appointment, eager to get it over with. As soon as we entered the examination room, we were privy to various sharp objects lying in wait on a tray. This has happened to me before, while anticipating gynecological procedures, but these tools seemed even more spectacularly medieval than the ones at the gyno. These bitches will cut your bones, I thought.

As the doc explained in horrifying detail what would be done, I zoned out. Please, just like put me in a K-hole and do whatever you need to do, I thought. I'd never done the drug K, but had been around others in its depressing, zombified state, that seemed about right for this procedure. After the tutorial, I laid down on my left side, where Kelli sat looking into my eyes as the doctor found a good spot on my right pelvic bone (i.e. my butt) to take the plunge. Needle pricks, local anesthetic, so far so good.

"I'm going to go into the bone now with some anesthetic. Believe me, you're going to want this," the doc said as if from a distance.

I winced.

Kelli offered, "You're doing great honey. I love you so much."

*WOW. THAT HURTS. ARE YOU F***ING SERIOUS!* I gasped, followed by tears.

"I'm sorry about this. You're doing great," the doc said. There was a short break, before she came at me with another implement. "Now I'm getting the marrow sample, going into the bone."

Less pain, thanks to the anesthesia, but incredible discomfort. More tears. Kelli kissed my forehead and the doc delved deeper into my bone.

"You're doing fantastic," both women said.
"I love you so much," Kelli added. "You're so beautiful."

An uncomfortable intimacy took over the situation, as if we were participating in a surprise three-way: My girlfriend caressing my face as the doc worked up a rhythm, her tool thrusting in and out of my backside.

Finally, she got what she was after, placed it in a specimen jar, where it formed a red globule, not unlike those in a lava lamp.

"Got it. Beautiful!" The doc said, holding it up. "Now I just need to get a tiny piece of bone."

Medical test boot camp completed, Cheryl received a diagnosis of Hodgkin's lymphoma. Medical people cheered. We cheered. It was the best case scenario. We learned that 87 percent of people with Hodgkins who received the standard care are completely cured. And although Cheryl's chest tumor was one of the biggest the oncologist had ever seen, we decided Everything Would Be Fine.

Cheryl had told some of her closest friends about the preliminary diagnosis, but she hadn't yet come out

to all of her crew. Once Cheryl was given a treatment schedule, I suggested we should start telling people. Not thrilled with this idea, she wrote:

I'm a relatively private person. This has often come into conflict with my writerly pursuits as a performance poet and memoirist. There's only so much of myself that I want to put out there and I wasn't sure if I wanted everyone to know I had cancer.

Since Kelli is a bit of a pro at caretaking, she explained it was necessary to let our friends know, so they could lend a hand. "They will want to help. We need to let them know how."

I wasn't so sure. Although I have many wonderful friends, others have left me gravely disappointed in my times of need. I also didn't want to burden anyone with my problems. Then there was the matter of pride: I like to be the one giving the help, not receiving it.

Kelli suggested she start an online community with a list of our needs; rides, food, company, etc. I agreed to this. Then we made the calls.

I wrote out a script for myself. If they picked up I would engage them in normal conversation at first, then slide into, "well, you probably know that I've been kind of sick for a while..." If it went to voice mail, I would say, "Hey there. It's Cheryl. Please give me a call when you get a chance. I'd like to tell you about something that's going on with me."

They all went to voice mail. As my friends called back throughout the day, I became more at ease telling each person, cracking jokes about my overachieving tumor and its melon namesake. Many of them were silent on the other end, I could imagine them staring into space, before they each said, "I don't know what to say."

This went on for a while, as I continued to move my friend Keith to the bottom of the "To Call" list. Keith had suffered through treatment for a rare form of Non-Hodgkin's lymphoma back in early 2001. I had helped take care of him through much of this, which, from just my caretaker's perspective seemed like an absolute ordeal, although effective; he has been in remission since. A decade later, I feared the same fate for myself.

I finally called Keith, leaving the voicemail spiel. When he called back shortly after, I launched into the pre-packaged convo that I'd been repeating for a few hours, "You know I've been sick for a while... Thought it was asthma, allergies at first... Turns out there's a large tumor in my chest... It's Lym..." I stuttered and tried again. "Lymp..." adrenaline surging, "Lym..." I handed the phone to Kelli. "It's Keith, you tell him please." I said. And she did, handing the phone back to me after passing along the info.

"Well, I'm here for you whatever it is," he said.

We said our goodbyes and I Love Yous and I turned off my phone. Kelli continued to chat, holding conversations longer than I was typically capable.

I escaped into a hot shower, looking down at my thinning body, amazed with the perkiness of my breasts. Damn, my tits look better now than ever, I laughed to myself, coming down from the adrenaline. But, seriously they did.

Having a well-honed sense of both irony and cynicism comes in handy sometimes. Like when you've never smoked, work out four times a week, eat practically vegan and you're the one in your family who ends up with cancer. Cheryl finally told her mother about her diagnosis. Later her mom visited and said "this shouldn't have been you, Cher, it shoulda been me. It shoulda been me. It shoulda been me."

She kept at it until Cheryl said "Ma, yes yes, of course it should have been you. Now shut up." Her mom, who allegedly gave up smoking after a medical scare in 2008, immediately began chain smoking again.

Cheryl started chemo and since she would soon lose her hair, our friend Diana suggested a preemptive "good ol' fashioned lesbian head shaving." Cheryl agreed:

> I'd never taken part in this particular ritual as such, but I used to shave the back of my shiny midnight black bob (it was the early '90s). I have also shaved many of my girlfriend's heads (again, the '90s). Anyway, I invited a handful of my Sapphic sisters over, cooked up a vat of vegetarian chili and made everyone sing "Closer to Fine," poorly, which seemed like a lesbian thing to do. First Kelli chopped off my ponytail, then Diana went to work on my head with the clippers as our friend Syd took photos, and several friends looked on. Yes, I was surrounded by some of the greatest queers of my generation, who are also superbly awesome friends.

Later, we showed photos of the Good Ol' Fashioned Lesbian Head Shaving to the nurses at the chemo suite. "Can we tell other patients about this?" they asked. Cheryl thought. "Of course, but tell them they have to call it the Good Ol' Fashioned Lesbian Head Shaving Ritual as well. Even if they're not lesbians."

Although the chemo immediately began to shrink Cheryl's cantaloupe-sized tumor, it also was doing her a serious number on her white blood cells, leaving her susceptible to infections. Her oncologist agreed to continue with the treatment but cautioned that Cheryl needed to avoid germy places which included, of course, the entire New York City subway system. We moved the party into our Sunset Park apartment and although Cheryl was extremely tired, we entertained a lot that winter. On December 23, 2010, Cheryl wrote:

I've been a bit overwhelmed, in a good way, at the love and support I've felt in the past few weeks. I have a truly fabulous, caring community of artists, nerds, queers, intellectuals, sober folks, weirdos, really cool straight people and performer types behind me. I really don't know what I'd do without you all.

Beloved, but dormant friendships have been rekindled. Current relationships have been strengthened. People have come out of the woodwork to wish me well. Fellow cancer patients have reached out to lend their suggestions and support. Cookies have been baked, food has been prepared. Rides have been offered. Folks have been taking care of Kelli as well, which enables her to take care of me. To put my well-honed cynicism aside for a moment, this experience has changed my perspective on asking for support and opening myself up to accepting it. you for helping me feel not so alone.

Smooches.

For Christmas, our friends chipped in and got us a huge gift certificate for a website that home delivers organic groceries. Cheryl was amazed "that would have never happened when I was drinking," she said, as we made our first shopping list, "I guess cokehead friends and chemo friends are pretty different."

From a New Year's Eve post, written a week later:

I'm not going to lie to you. 2010 was a crap year. My diagnosis sort of topped it off, but oddly brought along some fabulous side effects, including a renewed spark of creativity, and as I mentioned before, overwhelming support and love from my community. I'm thankful my treatment has been going well and as of this Tuesday, I'm a third done with my chemo. I'm thankful I'm not terribly sick or in pain or in despair. I'm thankful I have an amazing girlfriend by my side. I'm thankful my illness has allowed me to see the wonderful things around me clearer than ever.

We were still completely hopeful then. At the time, that made sense.

The standard treatment for Hodgkin's lymphoma, a treatment which has been in use since the '70s, is know by the common moniker ABVD. The B stands for bleomyocin. About 87 percent of people with Hodgkin's who receive this treatment are completely cured. Two out of one hundred people who get bleomyocin die from it. In fact, when experimenters need to give rats in the laboratory lung damage quickly, they expose them to bleomyocin.

In February 2011, Cheryl went in for a chemo treatment and reported feeling short of breath. Cheryl's oncologist said the onset was not quick enough for it to be related to the bleomyocin and that she was probably short of breath because she was anemic. Cheryl continued with her full dose of chemo that day. Later, tests showed that she was having a bleomyocin reaction. Cheryl eventually went on high dose steroids, but they didn't help much, and Cheryl was struggling more and more with even the simplest of daily tasks.

On April 5, 2011, Cheryl wrote:

My girlfriend wanted to take me to the hospital for our anniversary. Ok not "for" our anniversary but right around then and because I couldn't breathe. The girlfriend made all the calls: doc, friend to give us a ride, other friend to accompany us, she began to pack my bag.

I didn't stop her, afraid to leave the spot on my bed.

Here's a riddle: how does someone who can't stand or walk without losing all breath get down three flights of stairs to be driven to the ER? The answer is on her butt, cold marble through loose jeans, girlfriend coaxed by threats of 911. Friend tries to carry lung-issue girl on her back, but the floor is less of a challenge, a front-loaded crawl.

The building is quiet with TVs on someone is roasting a chicken.

My friends put me in an old wheelchair to get me out the door and we run into my neighbor who glides us into the street wearing a business suit.

Cheryl was admitted to the respiratory step down unit, and later had to be moved to the ICU. The bleomyocin had caused inflammation to her lungs and the continued inflammation was making her lungs fibrotic. The stiffer her lungs became, the harder it was for Cheryl to breathe.

Medical people weren't cheering now. They were avoiding our eyes and talking in hushed tones and asking what we thought were ridiculous questions about end-of-life decisions. One first-year resident asked what Cheryl wanted to do about ventilation while she was simultaneously examining her own split ends. Avoidance? Immaturity? Cheryl later suggested one of us punch her in the head. This did not seem altogether inappropriate.

Cheryl got worse and then better and then slowly worse again. She went to rehab for a time, and we cheered, believing this meant she would recover completely. Cheryl, I think, was not so sure. She couldn't eat, wasn't able to stand and was on continuous high-dose oxygen. One night at rehab when I crawled in bed to watch Animal Planet with her she said "I don't know how much longer I can do this" and then without further comment, turned her attention back to the lion eating the gazelle. I couldn't coax more out of her and it wasn't her final answer, perhaps, but she wanted me to know.

On June 16, 2011, Cheryl had to be re-admitted to Beth Israel's ICU. The bleomyocin had so severely damaged her lungs that each breath was a sustained effort and her chest rose and then fell like a board being dropped. She died in the very early morning of June 18 . While her death wasn't pretty, thanks to liberal amounts of morphine, it seemed as peaceful as it was ludicrous. As I took off her glasses which she insisted on wearing to her last moments of consciousness, I could imagine her rolling her eyes "I wasn't supposed to die of this shit, I was just supposed to get a book deal."

Over 300 of Cheryl's friends gathered on July 26, 2011, at Dixon Place, an alternative performance space in the Lower East Side, to celebrate her life and be pissed off that she was dead. It was a spectacularly unsentimental memorial service, funny and tough, as one friend observed, just like Cheryl. Her artist and performer friends read what they had selected as their favorite pieces of Cheryl's work. The choices, like the crowd, were eclectic and while it's probably rare that a funeral includes stories written by the deceased about giving blow jobs on the New Jersey turnpike, it was completely fitting for Cheryl.

KELLI DUNHAM
JUNE, 2012

Public Transportation

WRITTEN BY CHERYL BURKE
MARCH 2011

I KNOW YOU'RE A VERY IMPORTANT PERSON THAT'S GOTTA GET somewhere to do important things with other VIPs and the slack subway stair climb of my healthy-seeming body reminds you of human limitations and you don't like to be reminded of limits so you sigh, under your breath wondering, "what's wrong with this bitch?"

If I could I would look at myself sideways as well, holding onto the rail pulling myself up one stair, then another, as my chest seems to explode from within, toxic lung from chemo, my heart overcompensates for my defects, again.

A woman, I apologize too much. Say I'm sorry to inanimate objects and the dimwits behind me. Sometimes I hate this city.

In the morning, a girl rocks back and forth on the train, cool sneakers, blue nail color applied by an expert. I wonder about her condition. Could be a hangover or maybe a chronic illness. She walks from one pole to another, touching each one, perhaps OCD or staving off the spins. It all looks the same to me now. She still has on her a jacket and a cell phone, I'm glad to see. Let's hope her keys are in her pocket and she'll be all right.

MEMBERS OF CHERYL BURKE'S WRITING GROUP MADE SIGNIFICANT CONTRIBUTIONS TO THE COMPLETION OF THIS BOOK

ANNE ELLIOTT is a New York spoken word veteran with stage credits including PS122 and The Whitney Museum. She met Cheryl B in the early 1990's on the slam stage of the Nuyorican Poets Cafe, and collaborated with her and others on the funk/rock/talk album *Hot Sauce Gizzard's Live Poultry*. In more recent years, Elliott's fiction has appeared in the *Bellevue Literary Review, Hobart, The Normal School, r.kv.r.y*, and *FRiGG*.

VIRGINIA VITZTHUM is the author of *I Love You, Let's Meet: Adventures in Online Dating* and *My Blind Date Went Blind* (both workshopped in the writers' group with Cheryl). She has written for salon.com, *Elle, The Village Voice, AlterNet*, and many other publications. She edits *Represent*, a magazine by and for youth in foster care.

MARIA LUISA is a journalist and editor who has covered crime, courts, politics, mental health and housing for *The Village Voice, AlterNet*, and several other publications. These days, she directs a teen writing program at Youth Communication, a nonprofit publishing company that produces magazines and books for marginalized youth. She was a member of Cheryl B's writing group from 2009 to 2011.

CHERYL BURKE *(1972-2011)* was a journalist, poet, performer and playwright who came of age in the vibrant 1990s East Village art scene. Her performances at the Nuyorican Poets Café, Bowery Poetry Club, the National Arts Club, P.S. 122, St. Marks Poetry Project established Burke as a young luminary and during her career she performed at venues throughout the U.S. and abroad. Her work was published in *Ping Pong, BUST, KGB Bar Lit, Go Magazine, Velvet Park,* a dozens of other journals and magazines, and anthologized in *Word Warriors: 35 Women Leaders in the Spoken Word Revolution* (Seal Press, 2007), *Reactions 5* (Pen & Inc, 2005), *The Milk of Almonds: Italian-American Women Writers on Food & Culture* (Feminist Press, 2002), *The World in Us* (St. Martins Press, 2000), *Pills, Thrills, Chills and Heartache* (Alyson Books, 2004), *His Hands, His Tools, His Sex, His Dress* (Haworth Press, 2001), among others. Burke was a graduate of both New York University and The New School. She passed away at the age of 38 from complications related to treatment of Hodgkin's Lymphoma.

My Awesome Place is her first book.